Island War

PATRICIA REILLY GIFF

HOLIDAY HOUSE • NEW YORK

title page: Bonaparte's Gull

First Edition
1 3 5 7 9 10 8 6 4 2

Library of Congress Cataloging-in-Publication Data

Names: Giff, Patricia Reilly, author.
Title: Island war / by Patricia Reilly Giff.
Description: First edition. | New York : Holiday House, [2018]
Summary: "In 1942 Izzy and Matt become trapped on a Japanese-occupied
Aleutian Island when the rest of the American population is evacuated
and must survive on their own for the duration of World War II"—Provided by publisher.
Identifiers: LCCN 2017019228 | ISBN 9780823439546 (hardcover)
Subjects: | CYAC: Survival—Fiction. | Friendship—Fiction. | World War,
1939–1945—Alaska—Fiction. | Alaska—History—1867–1959—Fiction.
Classification: LCC PZ7.G3626 Isl 2018 | DDC [Fic]—dc23 LC record
available at https://lccn.loc.gov/2017019228

With love
To my husband, James Anthony Giff,
who believed in me,
and who was everything to me.

To my son, James Matthew Giff,
who shared love of family
and the world of books with me.

To my grandson, James Patrick Giff,
who was there for me
when I needed him most.

—1941—

Horned Puffin

ONE

Izzy

MY closet was empty, except for a pair of woolly pajamas I'd thrown in back with the dust balls. I'd never wear them in a hundred years.

Everything else was spread out: on the floor, the bed, even covering the scratched-up desk I never used. My warm jacket and boots were there, and a couple of pairs of knee socks, one with holes. My pink party dress with the velvet buttons was hanging off the lampshade.

"Izzy?" Mom called. "Isabel?"

"Coming," I said, half listening.

She must have thought I said "Come in." She opened the door, then leaned back against the wall. "Oh, Izzy. What are you doing?"

I sank down on the edge of the bed. "Packing, I guess. Just in case you change your mind."

"We can't go to the island. Not without Dad." Her blue eyes filled with tears. "It's so far," she said, almost thinking aloud. "A thousand miles stretched out from Alaska, the Bering Sea to the north, the Pacific to the south. Cold and foggy."

She reached for my hand. "And suppose war comes?"

What did I care about a war? Hadn't Dad said, "Oh, Izzy, my girl, you'd love the island, the snow, and the wind! You'd feel as if it would blow you across the fields, and over the mountain, and above the sea."

Dad had leaned forward, his elbows on the table. "Imagine. Eons ago, nothing was there but water. Ah, but underneath, a chain of mountains. Maybe they wanted to see the light. They inched up toward the surface and the water fell away. Now there were islands, Izzy. One of them was ours."

Dad had written dozens of books about adventure and travel. I'd read the one about that wild and mysterious island; I'd read the one about a land bridge that stretched from Asia to the island, and the people who traveled across, all those years ago. They settled on the island, loving it. It was eleven hundred miles from the main part of Alaska, and only about fifteen miles wide. I had to see it for myself.

"Dad wanted us to go, you know that. He made the

plans, times, and tickets," I said. "You'd see those birds you always talked about. You'd write about them."

And I could skip school. Imagine what that would be like! No ending up with Mrs. Dane for the second year in a row, fifth grade and now sixth. No book reports that would keep me sitting still, reading some boring story, for half the afternoon.

"Think about your notebook," I told Mom. It was filled with thoughts about birds: those that flew overhead here in Connecticut, and a list of those she wanted to see on the island.

She loved birds! Yesterday, she'd teetered on a ladder roof-high as she returned a house wren, nothing but fluff, to its nest.

I reached over to the night table and pushed a couple of books aside, summer reading that I hadn't done. Somewhere I had a picture of a special bird Dad had drawn.

Yes. I held it up. A bittern, yellow above, buff below, and long yellow legs. It must have come to the island, instead of staying in Indonesia where it belonged. "If a bittern lands there," I said, repeating Dad's words, "Mom will spot it."

"Dad . . ." Mom began; her mouth trembled.

I knew we were both thinking about him. How he'd loved Mom with her pillow shape, and my twelve-year-old self with my thick-as-a-bottle eyeglasses, my restless legs and arms.

That terrible day came back! *The truck barreling along the avenue, the driver looking out the side window...*

The truck screeching as it hit the curb, hit Dad.

Two months, thirteen days ago.

Stop!

I began to talk, to fill space. "We'd take trains and boats, zip across the country from Connecticut, all the way to the island, a thousand miles out from Alaska. The people there think you're coming. They have a house for us. And I want..."

A new place. Wind. Snow. Everything.

I reached for some of the other pictures Dad had taken with his box camera: plovers and teals perched on a ledge, the mouth of the cave where he'd listened to the roar of the ocean's surf, and watched snow sweeping sideways against the wind. He took pictures of places he loved and Gram had some of them framed in her bedroom.

Gram stood in the doorway now. "Go," she said, grinning at me.

Gram with her dark eyes and straight hair like mine. Gram, who poured orange juice into her cereal instead of milk: "Delicious, Izzy, try it," and stayed up every night to listen to the radio. "Who wants to waste time sleeping?" Gram who had lived with us forever and was more fun than anyone I knew.

Mom looked at Gram, and then at me. Her arm circled my skinny back. "We'd be starting over."

Just what I wanted. I waited.

Mom turned. "I guess…"

Behind her, Gram was nodding.

I hugged Mom hard. "Hurry," I said.

She and Gram went into the kitchen to talk things over, and I slid the summer reading books under the bed. Then I began to fill the suitcase. On the very top I put the pink party dress that Gram had made for me. It was cottony soft and I loved it. I couldn't leave it at home.

I slammed the suitcase shut and leaned on it so I could fasten the buckles.

I was ready!

TWO

MATT

OUT on Long Island Sound, I rowed hard, a wake churning up behind me. My hands were used to this, my palms callused. I dug in the oars, listening to the waves slap against the boat, and counted the strokes in my head.

Faster. Smoother.

I breathed in the salty air. School would begin next week, and the rowing competition after that. And Mom swam every day, getting ready for her swim meets. "We're getting better all the time," she'd say, smiling at me.

In the distance, a barge chugged its way toward the Atlantic. Then something made me turn. Pop was standing on the dock, hands on his hips, watching me.

Pop?

How had he gotten there? How did he even know where I was?

Mom and I hadn't seen him since he went on one of his trips weeks ago. And who knew what they were all about? He'd never said a word about where he'd been, or why.

So he was home!

The peace in the house was gone. He was always annoyed. *Did you take the garbage out, Matt? Your books are all over the place. Did you mow the lawn?*

I lowered my head, taking another stroke. From the corner of my eye, I saw his arm raised, motioning for me to come in to the wharf.

I used the left oar to circle around, then straightened out, moving toward him. Let him see I knew exactly what I was doing.

"Hey, Matt." He reached out to loop the boat rope around the hook. "News."

Drips of water plinking, I held the oars up, then shoved them back into the boat.

"We'll get a hamburger or something," Pop said, "and I'll tell you about it."

"Where's Mom?" I asked.

"Home. I wanted to talk to you myself."

I dragged the boat up onto a grassy spot, and then we walked back along the gravel path to the diner on the corner, his hand on my shoulder. Inside, he began to tell me what was going to happen.

To me!

"We're going to an island," he said. "American, but closer to Asia. The weather's not so hot, only eight or ten days a year are clear. The rest are rainy, foggy, and snow in the winter, of course. But we'll manage. It'll only be for a couple of months." He shrugged. "Maybe until spring."

I looked at him, horrified. "Spring! And Mom has swim meets all winter. How can she give all that up?"

He shook his head. "No, it'll just be you and me, the two of us."

Before I could think of what to say, the server came to take our order. Pop spoke for us both. "Hamburgers with onions."

I hated onions.

"Wait." I held up my hand.

How could I give up rowing, or cheering Mom on as she raced?

Most of all, how would it be to spend time with him on some island with not-so-hot weather? I knew what the answer to that was.

"What will Mom say?" I asked.

"She knows. I told her we need time together. Months, maybe."

The server slapped down our plates, everything smelling like onions. Pop took a bite. "Eat. It's pretty good."

I pushed the plate away. "You can't make me go," I said, knowing he could, of course he could. "I row every day. And what about school?"

"There'll be another school. And you might have a boat on the island. It'll be different, Matt. Things aren't always the way you think they are. It'll be the adventure of a lifetime."

I stared at my plate; the onions looked like small worms.

"Let me tell you about the island," Pop said. "The Aluets have been there for thousands of years. You love the water, and so do they. They fish for big catch in their kayaks. I want you to see that place. We'll get to know each other better. I want that too."

I didn't have a choice. Who knew what would happen to my own boat? I wouldn't watch Mom swimming. Everything in school would be normal. But not me.

I'd have to give it all up. Worse, I'd be with a father who was gruff and miserable, in a place I'd never heard of.

I swallowed. If I choked up, I could imagine what Pop would say.

I pulled the plate closer, managed to eat the hamburger slathered with onions, and stared out the window at the Sound.

THREE

Izzy

WE took one dusty train after another all the way across the country. A week? I'd lost count of the days. And then one ship after another.

But then, the last ship! We climbed aboard, on our way. We chugged toward the island, feeling the wind pick up and waves pitch the ship from side to side.

Mom went inside where it was warm, but I circled the deck, trying to keep my balance. I darted around boxes and jumped over loops of rope.

I didn't see the boy sitting against the railing, his huge feet stretched out in front of him, until it was too late.

I tripped over him and went down hard.

Scrambling up, I was ready to say *Sorry*. He pushed back his hair with hands the size of dinner plates and stared at me as if it were my fault.

Of course, it was my fault. My elbows were always scraped, and my knees had scabs as big as apples.

The boy glared. "Huh!" he muttered under his breath, but loud enough for me to hear.

Then I realized. I knew who he was. I'd seen him in the halls at school. He was a couple of classes ahead of me.

I slid behind a huge metal container and balled up my fists. "Watch out, kid," I whispered. Dad would have laughed. I didn't have the strength to fight off an ant, much less a kid who was ten times bigger than I was.

I stayed away from him for the rest of the trip, wiping the rain off my glasses so I could peer around corners at him.

When the island was close, Mom came outside. "Ah, look," she said as we heard birds honk overhead. "A pair of emperor geese."

I saw their white heads and dark bodies, but only for a moment. The rain had changed to sleet; it stung my face and spattered the waves that rose almost to the railing.

Imagine! Sleet in October.

How I loved it. I almost twirled off the gangplank, beating that kid off the ship. Mom followed, smiling, as the weather suddenly cleared.

The rest was a blur. There were only about forty people on the island. It seemed as if almost everyone was there. Women surrounded us, telling us their names and showing us the houses, our wooden cottage.

Inside were three rooms: chairs, a table, and a couch in one, two bedrooms in back. The bathroom was outside.

This would all be perfect except that from the window, I saw the kid from the boat, walking with a man who must have been his father. He stared in at me.

One of the women started a fire in the wood stove so we'd be warm. "Driftwood," she said over her shoulder. "We spend a lot of time at the water's edge looking for pieces to use." She shrugged. "Not one tree on the island. We have to import wood we need to build."

Baskets woven from dried grass were set up on a small table. A girl leaned toward me. "Don't look at the basket in back. It's mine, the first one I've done, and it's a little—" She broke off, looking anxious.

"It's beautiful," I breathed, looking at the small basket with a lid.

She grinned at me; her dark eyes crinkled as if they were smiling too.

I pushed my glasses up on my nose. "I'm Izzy."

"Maria," she said. "Come on."

Outside, she walked slowly along the gravel path,

while I had to hold myself back from racing to see every-thing: ryegrass blowing in the field, mountains in the distance that would be covered with snow this winter.

We passed houses huddled together, and Maria pointed to a white church. "If it weren't foggy, you could see the steeple. It almost reaches the sky."

Looking up, I nearly stepped on a large dog asleep on the path. "*Sabaakax*," Maria said. "Dog, in our old language."

I couldn't begin to pronounce that. But Maria went on. "He doesn't belong to anyone, so we all feed him."

I glanced after him, a mess of a dog with droopy ears and thick gray-and-white fur. I wished he belonged to me! I'd always wanted a dog I could race around with, a dog to cuddle up with on cold winter nights.

Maria locked her arm in mine, and we climbed a hill so steep, it made me breathless. "Thor Hill," Maria said as we reached the top. "Not its real name; I just call it that. I like to read about old myths, and Thor had some-thing to do with storms and thunder. Perfect for this place."

What would it be like to let myself go, arms out, to sail down the other side, the wind in my face? But my feet and legs were tired. I looked back toward the village. "A long walk," I said.

Maria grinned and waved her hand. "This is nothing. You'll get used to walking. It's miles to the ocean side. After a while your legs will toughen up."

It sounded fine; it sounded wonderful. I'd be able to walk along paths, to find my way . . .

"Wait," I began. "There was a cave . . ." I thought of Dad's words. *From the opening you can see kittiwakes and cormorants flying above, shrieking.* "My father spent a summer here once writing a book," I said. "He wrote about that cave."

She shook her head. "There are so many rocky places; it could be anywhere. There's a place I love on the other side of Thor Hill. Just an overhang under the rocks, but cozy. We'll go someday."

If only Dad were holding my hand, showing me where to go. But I'd find that cave. Miles would be nothing.

"Don't you love to read?" Maria asked.

Read? The last time I'd read a book I'd been conned into it by Dad. "Read a page for me every day," he'd said. "Just one."

I wished I had done that, wished I had read all of his books.

"Did you bring books?" she asked. "We could trade back and forth. I have *The Call of the Wild* and *A Girl of the Limberlost*. Oh, and one about myths and legends."

I was lost! I shook my head. "I didn't have room in my suitcase." At least that was the truth.

She gave my arm a shake. "Here comes that new boy."

He saw us, frowned, and turned back down the hill, but Maria wasn't paying attention. She pointed. "Across the sea to the north is Russia. This island used to belong to them. And Japan is southwest," she said. "They say we're going to have a war, but the American army might come to evacuate us."

Before I could think about it, she was asking what I'd read lately.

Outside of Dad's book, there wasn't one I'd ever finished. Just a title, I told myself desperately, even Dad's, but I couldn't even come up with that. I raised my shoulders and looked away as I saw her surprise.

The next day I started school. School after all! It was only a few doors down, but Mom and I hugged as if I'd be gone for days.

How strange to be in a class with only five other kids. It took only a few minutes to remember their names: Nick, Paul, Catherine, Maria, of course, and that boy: Matt.

Outside, the wind was strong; it rattled the glass panes and sent an empty box flying across the village. My feet were restless under me. If only I were out there, arms stretched like wings, flying along like the blue herons I could see in the distance.

In front, the teacher looked out as Mom went by, her notebook fluttering in her hand. "Long ago, there was no wind," Mrs. Weio began, pushing back her gray hair. "A woman longed for a child, so her husband carved a wooden doll for her. One night, the doll breathed, and the next, he was gone."

Maria whispered, "Mrs. Weio loves old legends."

Mrs. Weio raised her thin arms. "The doll punched through a hole in the sky ceiling, and wind blew in, bringing birds and animals with it. Happy, the doll went home to live."

The teacher smiled, lines deepening across her forehead. "And so we have wind, *williwaws!*"

I could imagine it: dogs, and cats, and bears, tumbling down to earth.

But outside at recess, no one talked about legends; they talked about war.

"It won't happen," Maria said.

The ship boy, Matt, stared at her. "You're wrong!"

I couldn't resist. "You think you know everything? You're not so perfect, you know."

He glared at me, then turned away.

That night, Mom and I wrapped ourselves in blankets and sat on the couch. She talked about plovers with their dark gray neck rings as we sipped tea and ate slippery oysters that someone had left in our doorway.

For the first time, I was uneasy. Was that miserable boy right? Was war coming?

Would it happen here?

It was too much to think about.

FOUR

MATT

I was back in school, a month late. How strange it was: only six of us. The fresh kid from the ship was there. I remembered seeing her at home once or twice.

I looked around. The classroom was ordinary. The alphabet, white letters on dusty black paper, was tacked up near the ceiling, and a map was rolled down on the board. Instead of a picture of George Washington hanging in front, there was one of a man with a fat face and a moustache. The teacher liked to talk about him: Vitus Bering, who had explored some of the islands.

I stared out the window. The sky was a sheet of gray. I tried not to think about home, the Sound sparkling in the fall sun and the leaves turning red and orange.

Home.

I bit my lip. How would I ever get used to this desolate place? And how would I get used to missing Mom?

We'd talk about races, swimming, rowing, while we ate dinner. It was what we thought about all the time.

Izzy, the girl from the ship, sat near the window. Behind her thick glasses, her eyes looked like a pair of fish swimming in a bowl. She never sat still, feet moving, hands tapping.

I still had a bruise on my foot from where she'd dug into me on the ship.

Someone to stay away from!

After school, an older boy from the village waited outside for me. A teenager, I guessed. "You're Matt?" he asked.

"Sure."

"I'm Michael. Your father asked me to show you a *baidarka*."

Now what!

Pop had been a little better since we left. Not so irritable. Quiet, though. We'd eat at the table, neither of us talking. I reminded myself a dozen times that Mom had said he'd been a soldier, disciplined and mostly silent: a job he loved, until he hurt his knee and that life was over.

There was something else about him. Something he was doing here. Studying weather, was what he said.

But why? All you had to do was look out the window to see mist, and fog, and sometimes a rain squall.

I followed Michael down to the harbor. The surf boomed; huge waves smashed up against the pier. It was really cold, with the wind coming in from the sea.

"Your father wanted you to have a kayak," Michael said over his shoulder. "I'll show you . . ."

I couldn't believe it, but there it was, long and sleek, with sea lion skin stretched across the frame.

"One cockpit, just enough room for you," Michael said. "The opening is covered by a spray deck so water won't get in when you turn over. You'll right yourself in a moment."

Turn over?

I glanced out at the waves fighting each other. He was out of his mind. And he wasn't worried about my drowning. He grinned at me.

"A boy has to build a kayak before he can marry," he said. "I made my first one when I was sixteen."

He handed me a paddle. "Go ahead, try it."

I'd probably be floating in that water in a few minutes: choking, drowning.

I slid down into the opening, pushed off, and turned; a wave high over my head rushed toward me.

The kayak rose up, tilted, and I was underneath a wall of water; it filled my mouth, my nose. I couldn't breathe. I dug with the paddle, a green world around me. Swallowing water. Tasting salt.

I spun through a dark world, then up, alive. Freezing. Grabbing the paddle floating beside me.

I was furious at Pop. At Michael. At everyone.

FIVE

Izzy

I spent most of one day with Maria. "You'll be able to make a basket like the rest of us," she said. Maria's mother nodded. "You'll see, Izzy."

Outside Maria and I gathered long strands of grass. She bowed her head, then looking down at the field. "Thank you," she said, "for letting us have some of your grass."

So I bowed my head too, and echoed *thank you*. But from the corner of my eye, I saw the boy, Matt, staring at us. I frowned, trying to ignore him. He was always there when I didn't want to see him.

Back at Maria's we laid the grass on the table, and her mother brought in a glass of water. I raised it to my mouth. Thirsty or not, I didn't want her to think I wasn't grateful.

But Maria laughed. "We have to wet the grasses as we work. It's too hard to work with it dry."

We started to work then, twisting, braiding. I was

amazed to see it working. I could picture the basket finished, the grass a warm, tan color by then. Maybe I'd bring it home to Gram one day.

Gram. It was the end of November. She'd be cooking turkey for Thanksgiving, but Mom and I would have salmon instead. I felt a quick pain in my chest thinking of Gram so far away. But then I shook my head. She wanted us to be here.

I awoke on an early December morning to a world of snow. It covered the gravel path and blew in clumps against the window. I nudged Mom, who was still asleep. "I have to go out there."

She opened her eyes. "No birds for me today, honey. I think I'll stay in bed for just another..." Her eyes closed.

I pulled on boots, my jacket, and the blue beret Maria had given me, and I was out the door. The dog was there too, chasing his tail, then shaking the snow off his back. I wanted to pet him, but already he was galloping across the field, sending up a shower of white behind him.

Raising my face to the sky, I felt flakes on my cheeks and coating my glasses. The mountains were shadows in the distance now. Where would Dad's cave be?

I realized I wasn't alone. Mrs. Weio stood in front of the school. When she saw me, she came closer. "Don't you love the winter?" she called.

I nodded, feeling a little shy. I hadn't really talked to her in all the weeks we'd been on the island. She was kind, though, and didn't seem to mind my feet tapping under the table, or my wandering to the window to sharpen my pencil.

"We haven't gotten to know each other yet," she said, "but you remind me of your father."

I wiped my glasses and stared at her. She knew Dad? My words tripped over each other. "He was here, I know that. He wrote about a cave."

Mrs. Weio nodded. "I remember. He always had a book under his arm."

I didn't want to talk about that. She must know by now that I didn't like to read. "Did you know about the cave?" I asked.

"I did," she said. "It was deep, and there was a stream inside."

"But where?"

"I saw it once," she said. "I went there with him. He wanted to learn about the island, and we became friends."

I took it all in. "Could you tell me more?"

"The cave," she said. "I could see the beach, the surf, so it was along the ocean, high up, though. You'll find it if you keep looking. Yes, you'll find it. You're filled with energy."

She frowned, thinking. "There are two large rocks in the water, almost shaped like people. It's easier to see them when it's calm. It seems as if they're bowing to each other." She broke off. "You may have to hurry. I think we'll be at war and maybe..."

I didn't find out what she meant about maybe, because Matt was trudging up the path toward us. I gave her a quick wave and scurried away.

I didn't want to see him; I didn't want to think about him. We'd almost had a huge to-do, as Gram might say, after school yesterday. I'd been coming down the steps outside, and he just wouldn't get out of my way. He stood there, back toward me, talking to someone, and took a step to one side to block my path.

"Get out of my way," I said, hands raised. To give him a push? Not really, but he deserved it.

He turned and saw my hands. He stepped back then. "Ooh, I'm afraid," he said.

"You should be!"

The boy he'd been talking to laughed, and Matt laughed too.

I'd never met anyone so mean.

But right now, I wasn't going to get involved in another fight. I shook the snow off my shoulders and went back inside to have breakfast with Mom.

SIX

MATT

I stamped around my bedroom, finding boots, sweaters, a leather jacket. An icy rain slashed across the village, making it hard to see. It was starting out to be a horrible December.

At home, Mom would be getting ready for winter too, swimming at the Y, but not a winter like this. I shook my head. It was hard to think about Mom so far away.

But the *baidarka!*

"The sea is the sea," Pop had said. "No matter where you are."

It was true. I'd become good at speeding along in the kayak. I wasn't bad at navigating in these icy waters, the ins and outs of the coast that led to the beach, and the rocks above. I even knew how to right the boat quickly after a few tumbles.

I remembered Dad's irritable words: *Things aren't always the way you think they are.* Sometimes he might be right.

It was Sunday. I'd have all day out on the sea.

I passed Pop's bedroom door and called in. "Going in the kayak."

"Wait," he said.

I opened the door, just a crack, for the first time. His room was much neater than mine, the blanket stretched tight across the bed, his clothes hung on the hooks instead of lumped over the chair.

He turned, covering something in front of him. "What are you doing?" I asked.

"Never mind that," he said. "You can't go out on the water today."

It was always something with Pop. What did he think I was going to do? Hang around here all day?

"War," he said. "The Japanese bombed an island in the Pacific a little while ago."

"Here?"

Pop shook his head. "No, it was in Hawaii. The damage was terrible, our American ships sunk, half our fleet maybe, a lot of lives lost."

"But not us," I said again, reassuring myself. "So I'll go out—"

"Outside, all right. But stay out of that kayak today. Let's see what's going to happen."

I grabbed the door and slammed it shut again.

SEVEN

Izzy

THE day after the bombing in Hawaii, people stood in front of the school talking, worrying. Someone said, "But it's more than two thousand miles away."

The village chief came out of his house. "I've just heard," he said, his voice strained. "The president has declared war on Japan."

Mrs. Weio frowned. "We'll be evacuated by the American army before the war comes to us. We'll have to be ready to move fast."

The old grandmother from next door raised her arms in the air. Her face was filled with deep lines. Her dark eyes flashed. "You think the army will come here for us? They'll have more important problems." She pulled a woolen scarf over her head and stamped up the path and into her house.

I felt a catch in my throat. How terrible it all was.

I had to move away from them. I looked at Mom and pointed toward Maria's Thor Hill.

I ran, climbing, stopping to throw my arms around that gray-and-white dog sitting on a rock.

I could hardly see everybody below. Snow came down, faster every minute, covering my head. I could imagine, though: Mom standing there, still with her notebook in her hand, probably feeling guilty that she'd brought me here to the island.

But I didn't want to be evacuated. I didn't want to go back to Connecticut, back to Mrs. Dane.

I loved Mrs. Weio, who read to us and told us stories. And once she'd said, "Everyone has to find the right book to fall in love with reading." It was hard to believe that, but I was glad she'd said it.

I wasn't going to think about the bombing anymore. I raised my arms in the air.

But suppose . . . just suppose it came here!

EIGHT

MATT

WHAT would Mom have said about this Christmas? At home she always strung lights on an evergreen tree that smelled of winter. She covered it with ornaments and tinsel. Presents were piled up underneath!

I gritted my teeth. There was no tree, of course, not a tree on the whole island. No presents. Pop didn't even seem to realize it was Christmas Day.

He spent most of it holed up in his bedroom, the door shut tight.

Shrugging on my jacket and hood, still damp from the icy waves yesterday, I felt anger rise up in my throat. No, more than that: it was fury!

I went to his door and yelled in, "Merry Christmas!" and then I slammed out the front door, listening with satisfaction to the noise it made.

I stopped on the gravel path. What was he doing in there, anyway?

I pulled off my gloves and reached down for a handful of gravel. The pieces were sharp and freezing cold against my palms. The pain of it actually felt good, I was that furious.

I trudged around the back to look in his window. He'd hung a blanket across the glass, tight all around.

Almost all around.

I stood there, looking carefully at the blanket's hem. One corner was frayed, the wool in narrow strips.

I moved closer to peer inside. I couldn't see much: the bottom of the bed, a chair he'd pulled in from the other room, his feet against the rungs.

But that was all.

What was he staring at?

No matter how I angled my head, I couldn't tell.

I clenched the gravel with my fingers, standing there in this miserable place . . .

And threw it against the wall of the house as hard as I could, then began to run.

He came outside, calling my name.

I didn't turn. I didn't want to hear what he had to say.

I just wanted to escape from this day, even though I couldn't escape from the island.

–1942–

Emperor Goose

NINE

Izzy

EXCEPT for missing Dad, I'd never been so happy. Christmas morning, Mom had surprised me with a charm bracelet hung with tiny silver birds, and a pair of rolled-up gloves with furry insides.

"It was all I could fit in the suitcase," she'd said.

I wore the bracelet every day and wouldn't go out of the house without those warm gloves.

War hadn't come to us, even though people shook their heads, worried after the island of Guam fell.

But we were safe. At least for now.

Soon it was spring again. I'd finished another island-style basket which I'd given to Mom for her birthday.

One morning, Maria stood outside our house, a book under her arm, as always. "Let's climb the cliffs and watch the gulls swoop in. They're beginning to nest."

We slogged through the field over stones and mud, the mountains in front of us.

Maria stopped. "Wait."

She broke off a long sticklike plant and waved it in front of my nose. "Hey, Izzy, it's poison!"

She peeled down the outside and took a huge bite of the pale green inside. "Arghh," she moaned, and threw herself down on a rock.

I swiveled around, ready to run for help. But she was up, laughing. "Just the outside. The inside is delicious. Wild celery. Try some."

I put my hands in front of me. "No, thanks."

Still laughing, we reached the top of the cliff and rested on our elbows, watching the gulls. Maria looked up as a bird flew over our heads. "I never saw one like that before."

I glanced up too, but there was just a flash of color, a whirr of wings, before it was gone.

"In a couple of weeks, we can hold each other's legs and take turns. We'll steal an egg, just one, from each nest. The poor birds can't count; they'll never know we're taking their almost chicks."

Dangle over the edge?

Why not? I could do that.

"And berries!" she said. "The juice is so sweet; we'll eat dozens of them."

Wispy bits of mist lifted here and there, almost like smoke. I stared out at the water, watching the waves curl up and over on themselves, listening to their hiss and boom. Dad must have stood somewhere up high, hearing them too.

A gull flew high and dropped a shell that smashed on the rocks below, then dove down to eat the meat inside.

I shaded my eyes; my glasses were filthy. "A ship is out there, but I can't see the flag. Can you?"

"American, of course," Maria said. "But not to evacuate us. I think they've forgotten all about that. They're probably too lazy to raise the flag on a Sunday."

And then I said it aloud. "Sunday, Maria!"

We stared at each other, hands over our mouths.

Church. We'd forgotten all about it.

My shoes were a mess, my hair in knots. And Maria didn't look any better.

We brushed off our knees, straightened our hair, and ran, sliding, racing through the mud, and, heads down, sneaked into the last pew.

Mom turned, eyebrows raised when she saw me. I grinned at her, shrugging, and grabbed up the hymnal.

She grinned back, running her hand over her forehead, motioning to me to wipe the dirt off mine.

The sermon seemed too long for a gorgeous day, with sunlight beginning to splash in from the stained-glass windows, lighting the walls and the altar in reds and blues and even purples.

I swung my feet, impatient to be outside. It was the perfect day for exploring.

The moment church was over, Maria and I tiptoed down the aisle; we were first outside on the wooden steps.

I bent down to give the gray-and-white dog a quick pet, wishing for the hundredth time that he were mine. But when I told Maria that, she said he belonged to everyone.

It was clear enough now to see the ship's flag in the harbor: not the stars and stripes, but white with a huge red sun in the center.

Soldiers, dozens of them, stood on the path in front of the church.

For a moment, they didn't move. It almost seemed as if they were listening to the music still coming from the tiny organ inside.

But they weren't listening.

They began to shoot.

TEN

MATT

UP late, we hadn't gone to church this morning. Still half dressed, we were sitting in the kitchen when we heard a *pop-pop* sound, then the shattering of glass in the living room.

Pop reached out with one hand, pushing my head down hard on the table, just missing my plate.

"Slide underneath," he said.

I didn't stop to think. I did what he said, feeling my heart pound.

Had war finally come? Was Pop right when he'd told me it would happen sooner or later?

He sat on the floor next to me. "In a minute," he said, "I'll crawl into the bedroom. There's something I have to do. I want you to stay here."

"I'm coming with you."

He shook his head. "I have to hide"—he shrugged—"a radio." He reached out and grabbed my arm. "I have a place for it under the floorboards. If something happens to me, you'll have to get rid of it right away. If enemy soldiers find it . . ."

My mouth went dry. A radio, of course, in his room all this time! Suppose soldiers did find it? What would happen to us?

Pop must have seen how frightened I was. "Don't worry," he said. "I knew this was coming. I'm prepared for it."

I wasn't going to stay there under the table while he moved toward the bedroom. I followed him on my hands and knees. He was irritable and impatient, but I believed him. He was prepared. I wasn't alone. For the first time, I thought of the kayak. He'd made sure I had the boat, trying, I guess, to make things better between us.

Now I was so glad to have him there.

We lay flat on the bedroom floor, listening to bullets ripping into the wooden walls. Pop was under the bed, dragging out the radio.

I glanced under to see him lift floorboards, push the radio underneath, and close the wooden slabs over it. "Safe for now," he said.

There was no time for more. We heard a loud cracking sound as the front door splintered.

A soldier stood there. "Out!" he shouted.

ELEVEN

Izzy

MARIA and I scrambled back inside the church, smashing into each other. Someone was crying. In front of me, someone else was screaming over and over: "I knew it would happen, I knew there'd be an invasion!"

I saw Matt and his father come inside, a soldier carrying a rifle in back of them. A few minutes later, I heard the dog, still outside, whining.

Poor dog!

I reached back and opened the door a few inches. The dog pushed it farther with his nose. He padded inside and stood in the aisle, shaking.

Mom reached for me, her warm hands on my shoulders. She pushed me under a pew and crouched down, almost covering me.

The dog followed and lay next to me. I put my hand on his back as we listened to the sound of firing, the crackle of glass breaking.

I shoved my glasses into my pocket and covered my eyes with my hands. I didn't want to see what was happening. What might happen next!

My fist went to my mouth as I heard someone call out, "Stop! We're not armed!" Maria's mother whispered, "Please, please..."

For the first time, I thought we didn't belong here on an island, we should be in Connecticut, where there were no guns, no enemy soldiers.

At last, the firing stopped. Inside, the village chief was saying, "Calm. Try to be calm, everyone."

None of us moved. I'd never been so afraid.

We lay there for hours, wondering what would happen next. Mom's arm was heavy on my shoulders and there wasn't enough room to stretch my legs. Pins and needles shot through my hands and feet.

But Mom kept whispering, "We'll be all right, Izzy. I know we will."

Mom never lied. I knew she believed it. But I was sure she was wrong.

The day wore on, with nothing to eat, nothing to drink. I saw Matt standing in back with his father.

Then the door scraped open.

Mom's arms tightened around me.

"Out!" a soldier shouted. "All out now!"

No one moved. The village chief came down the aisle, calling to us. "We'll have to do as the soldier says."

I reached for my glasses as one by one we stood and followed him past soldiers who lined the path. They waved their rifles, pointing at the houses.

Were we free to go inside?

I glanced at the dog, who was running up the hill, and then at our own house, at bare openings where windows had been; at the pockmarked wooden walls.

But yes, that was what they wanted. Mom and I went up the path slowly, in case they changed their minds.

One of them looked angry; another looked as if he didn't care what happened to us. A third one nodded at me as I tripped over a stone, but I looked down quickly, not sure of what that meant.

Our neighbors moved slowly, the village chief helping the old grandmother hobble up her steps. She looked back and furiously waved her cane at the soldiers.

It almost seemed as if one of them, a man with a smooth face and a thin moustache, smiled.

Mom opened our door. All the food that had been neatly stored in boxes was gone. The beautiful baskets that had been made for us lay on the floor, crushed. In the bedroom, pillow feathers drifted in the air like snow; the blankets and sheets were scattered around, full of holes.

"Water." Mom pointed at the large jug in the corner that somehow had escaped ruin.

We found two glasses and drank; the water dribbled down my chin and neck. I wet my cheeks with my dirty fingers.

"Think of the cherry blossom trees in Washington," Mom said, "a gift from the Japanese people."

I thought of Dad smiling at Mom: *You always think of the good side of everyone.*

I sank down on the floor, my stomach gurgling from the water, but still so hungry. I began to cry, and Mom sat next to me, putting her arms around me, holding me close. She began to sing a song she loved, "I'll Get By."

And stopped, holding up her hand. "I know where there's food," she said. "At least, I think it might be still there."

She knelt, reached under the bed for her purse, and pulled out a small bag of raisins. She must have tucked it inside when we'd left Connecticut so long ago.

"A good omen," she said, tearing the bag open.

We ate, licking our fingers. Mom ate less than I did,

trying to give me more, so I tried to hold back, but it was hard to do.

She put the bag on my lap, then brushed my hair and straightened my glasses. "Dear Izzy," she said, and I reached out to put my arms around her wide waist.

The wind blew in through the shattered windows, a *williwaw*, strong and fierce.

"We'll go to sleep now; things always look better in the morning," Mom said. "We won't think of anything more tonight."

But I couldn't stop thinking. Soldiers with blank faces. Guns. Bayonets. What if . . .

What if . . . Mrs. Dane had said it a hundred times a day. *That's how you begin a story. That's how history might have been changed.*

Forget about Mrs. Dane and her what-ifs.

Think of the gulls flying. Think of hiding in Dad's cave, all of us, Mom and Mrs. Weio, Maria and her family.

If only I could find it.

TWELVE

MATT

I dreamed I was home in Connecticut. It was a rainy day, but that didn't matter. I was in the rowboat, oars up, head back.

I opened my eyes. It was still dark, probably the middle of the night. Soldiers were outside somewhere. And a radio was hidden under the floor.

What would Mom think if she knew what had happened? I was afraid and homesick. I felt it in my chest, in my throat.

The only time I was happy here on the island was when I was out on the sea in the kayak, the *baidarka*. Sometimes the mist was so strong the island was hidden and ghostly; it seemed like a different world, not at all the way it really was.

Pop would say I was feeling sorry for myself.

Yes, I was. Anger bubbled up.

Suppose I took the kayak out?

Impossible.

But I knew the small coves, the rocky shores; I knew this island.

Pop had secrets. So I'd have secrets.

Against Pop.

Against the soldiers.

Against everyone on this whole miserable island.

I leaned back against the pillow, figuring it out. I'd have to get the boat from the shed before it was light, before the soldiers saw me, before Pop figured out what I was doing.

The kayak was light. I'd hold it over my head, not making a sound as I went toward the water

It could be done.

Why not?

I slid out of bed and grabbed my jacket and boots. I took my time, moving slowly. After all, Pop was in the next room, his bed next to the wall between us.

I opened the door just a little and looked out to see what was happening. A soldier marched along the front path. He disappeared as he passed the house, but I heard his footsteps as he kept going.

I'd have to be quick before he came back this way. I

put my leg over the sill and climbed out, dashing down the alleyway toward the shed.

I slipped inside, hearing myself breathe, trying to be calm. The kayak was in front of me. I could feel the sea lion skin, stiff against my fingers.

As I raised the boat up, I listened; I heard a night bird, but the soldier wasn't coming after me. I opened the door farther, an inch at a time, until there was room to move the kayak.

Amazing. I didn't pass a soldier, or even see one, all the way to the harbor. I slid the kayak into the water and paddled through the rough waves in the dark, thinking of the best place to hide the boat.

A place I could get to when things were too much. A place to be peaceful.

I should have been paying more attention to what was going on around me. I should have been listening. Instead, I didn't hear anything unusual in the sound of the waves booming against the shore, until the motor-boat was almost on top of me: a boat filled with four men, with the enemy!

I took a huge breath, leaned to the side of the kayak, my whole body into it, leaned hard. *Turn over,* I thought desperately. *Turn over now.*

Above the surf, above the sound of the motor, I heard one of the men shout. They'd seen me!

That was my last thought before I felt the shock of the freezing water, before I swallowed a huge gulp of it.

I didn't try to right myself until there was no air left inside me, until I couldn't stay under for another moment.

I pushed, turned, and I was up, coughing. It was moments before I could breathe easily again.

The motorboat was gone, somewhere in the mist. Who knew what they thought? Where they were searching?

But there was the cove I was looking for. I was shivering, my teeth chattering. I slid the kayak in, fastened the rope to a small heavy rock, and sat there as the boat slid up and down in the waves.

A rim of light came from the east, almost morning.

I stepped out of the kayak, climbed the rocks, and rushed back to the house, trying not to make a sound. Inside, I hurried out of my wet clothes, cleaning the drops on the floor before Pop knew what I'd done.

Before anyone knew.

THIRTEEN

Izzy

WE'D slept in the same bed that night, Mom on the outside, me against the wall, our heads on the flattened pillows. I couldn't stop shivering, but after a while, I closed my eyes and dreamed of Dad standing in a cave near the top of a mountain, plovers flying over his head.

Morning came, filling the room with wisps of fog, and the sounds of shouting outside. I tried not to think about how frightened I was, and how hungry.

I crawled over Mom, who was still sleeping, and onto the floor. A small shard of glass sliced into my bare foot.

Nothing, I told myself, *it hardly even hurts*, even as I heard Mrs. Dane's voice, *Slow down, Izzy*.

I pulled out the glass and held my foot tight until the drops of blood disappeared. I slid into my shoes and went into the kitchen, closing cabinet doors, as I walked on one side of my foot.

By this time, Mom was up. She stood behind me,

running her hands over my shoulders. "We have to make the best—" she began.

There was a tremendous banging on our door.

We looked at each other. I could see terror in Mom's eyes, feel my heart ticking up into my throat.

We threw on our clothes while the furious banging went on.

Mom touched the top of my head. "Stay in the bedroom, Izzy."

I nodded and sat on the bed, my feet tapping, my hands clenching. If only Dad were here with us.

We both heard those words again: "Out!"

Slowly I went to the door. People stood in front of their houses, and one of the soldiers began to speak. "The men will fish today as normal."

As if anything might be normal.

"Some of us will go with them," he said. "The others will remain here."

The fishermen went forward. Maria cowered behind one of the house posts, and the old grandmother next door leaned on her cane, her wrinkled face filled with anger.

A toddler escaped from his mother and darted across the path toward the soldiers. "Peter, come back!" she called after him frantically, afraid to follow. After a moment, she took a chance, running to scoop him up as the soldiers watched.

I turned to go inside with Mom but glanced at the men as they went toward the dock, Matt walking along next to his father.

In the living room, Mom and I tried to straighten the baskets, but they were ruined. We swept aside the last bit of glass and sat close together on the floor in our jackets. It felt safer to be there than to be sitting on chairs where the soldiers could stare at us through the square openings that used to hold the windows.

Would the soldiers feed us? How could I even think of food? I couldn't help it, though; I felt my stomach turning over.

Mom reached for her notebook and paged through, talking about a Laysan albatross she had seen hovering over the water, its head snow-white and its wings so dark they were almost black.

"If something happens to me..." she began.

What if... "No!" I raised my hand to cover her mouth. I'd be alone. What would I do?

"It won't." Her voice was muffled. "But I want to be sure you'll see the birds for me."

I couldn't answer. I just nodded. It would never happen, I told myself fiercely.

But if it did...

Maria, I told myself. The teacher. The old grandmother. I whispered names over and over. They'd keep me safe.

I thought of Gram hugging me. When would I ever see her again?

I looked over at Mom, her round face, freckles spattered across her cheeks. What would I ever do without her?

FOURTEEN

MATT

FISHING today! We stumbled along toward the fishermen's kayaks. I'd been asleep only for an hour or two, but the williwaw was strong against my face and I began to wake up.

Pop looked exhausted. He put his arm around my shoulder, something he'd never done before. I was surprised at how I felt, a rush of warmth, even of love that I didn't even know I had for him.

But then I told myself I'd be home now, out on the Sound, if he hadn't made me come with him.

One of the fishermen beckoned. His kayak was long, with cockpits for three of us. He slid a large net onto hooks at the boat's stern to store the fish we'd catch.

I stepped down into one of the openings, watching Pop in front of me, moving quickly, as the fisherman held the boat steady.

We pushed off, the fisherman shouting, "Do you know how to paddle?"

"Sure," Pop said.

I was beginning to think he could do anything, feeling proud in spite of myself.

The waves slapped against the kayak as we moved toward the fishing grounds. Above us gulls were flying toward the island, maybe to nests on the cliffs.

In other times, the fishermen might have tried for a large catch, seals maybe. Michael had told me that when they were looking for a big fish like halibut, several kayaks would go out together. The men would cross paddles from one boat to another, to keep them steady. But today, I guessed, we needed a fast catch, a sure catch. The whole village had to be fed. Moments later, Pop caught the first fish; it looked like the fluke that we used to catch in the Sound.

At the same time, I saw my kayak, riding in the waves, plainly visible to anyone out on the water. Suppose Pop saw, or even the soldiers?

I'd have to move it as soon as I could.

We drifted away and, relieved, I raised my rod a little, waiting for a nibble.

FIFTEEN

Izzy

THAT night, a soldier shot his gun toward the sky. "Outside!" he shouted.

We walked to the schoolhouse, where the fishermen were spreading their nets. We could see the fish, stiff and white, their eyes staring and clouded over.

A few of the soldiers took most of the fish toward their tents in the back field. The village chief divided the rest carefully, whispering, "Sorry, so little," and at our turn, gave Mom and me two small fish.

The dog wandered around, looking up at all of us. Such a big dog! He must be starving.

Who could give up the only food we'd had all day?

I could. I had to. I tore off a small chunk of my share and gave it to him as a soldier with the pencil-thin moustache watched curiously.

Did he nod? It happened so quickly I couldn't be sure.

*   *   *

Early the next morning, I met Maria. There wouldn't be school today, and the men would go out fishing in an hour or two.

Matt was wandering around in back of the houses.

"Hi," I managed. Maybe it was time to forget about fighting now that we were at war.

He didn't answer but took longer steps, moving away from us.

"Another war," I muttered to Maria. "Battle after battle."

Matt looked over his shoulder, then headed toward Thor Hill. Two soldiers stood next to the path, talking to each other. They hadn't even noticed him.

What they did notice was my tripping over a rock, reaching for Maria, and nearly making her fall. One of them shook his head.

I felt the heat of Maria's arm even through her coat. Her face was flushed.

"What's the matter?" I asked her. Was it a rash I saw on her cheeks? "I think you're sick." I helped her, walking with her past my house, and her mother came to their door.

Her hands went to her face. "Oh, Maria," she said, and helped her inside.

Mom was on the teacher's step, talking, but I went back to our dark house. Friendly neighbors had covered the window openings with slabs of driftwood.

I left the door open for light, thinking of Maria. Did she have measles? Scarlet fever?

And what was Matt doing? Was he going to the cliffs to gather gulls' eggs to eat? Or maybe he'd gone to one of the beaches to dig for clams.

I thought of doing the same thing. But Mom had been very clear. "Don't go far, Izzy," she'd said. "Stay right here."

And that was what I had to do.

Maybe.

SIXTEEN

Izzy

THE men brought home fish for us every night, and the dog always stood near me, knowing I'd share a little with him. The soldier with the moustache watched.

From the doorway one afternoon, I saw two soldiers begin to string wires in back of our houses, looping them around posts they'd hammered into the soil.

They were locking us in. No one would be able to leave the village except the fishermen, and they were watched closely.

One day, the old grandmother hobbled down her path. "Go home where you belong!" she shouted at the soldiers, pointing her broom at them, almost as if it were a gun.

One of them pulled his rifle off his shoulder and raised it toward the sky.

"You don't belong on our island!" she kept shouting, until Mrs. Weio took her arm and led her back into the house. The soldier with the moustache began to smile, but when he saw me staring at him, he stopped, his face stern.

But I had to smile too. That old woman, hair escaping from her bun, bent and rail-thin, wasn't afraid of anything.

Mom was sitting at the kitchen table going over her notes, and I pressed her shoulder. "I'm going outside. All right?"

Mom squeezed my hand. "Not far."

I walked along the backs of the houses, peering at the soldiers' camp on one side of the wires and the yellow flowers blooming just beyond my reach.

A black bird, her neck ringed with white, startled up and flew over my head. Mom had pointed one out to me the other day. "A killdeer," she'd said, reaching for her notebook. "When she's nesting she'll flutter along the ground, pretending she has a broken wing, to lure intruders away."

I heard something and turned to peer over my shoulder. A soldier stood there, leaning on his rifle.

The dog appeared next to me and began to dig a hole under the fence. I glanced up at the soldier. How unfriendly he looked! I put my arms around the dog and tried to pull him back, afraid that the soldier would shoot.

But the dog kept digging, and then he was through, bounding across the field filled with flowers. He disappeared near Thor Hill.

I raised myself up on my hands, edged away from the fence, and walked to the back of Maria's house. Reaching up, I saw that she'd broken off a tiny piece of wood that covered her window. I peered inside.

She lay in bed with quilts covering her to her chin. Next to her was the pile of books that she brought to school every day.

I put my mouth close to the opening. "Maria?" I whispered.

She didn't move.

I knocked on the wood gently, and her eyes fluttered open. "It's me, Izzy, at the window."

She pushed herself up to lean against the back of the bed. Her face was flushed and her voice raspy as she said my name.

"What is it?" I asked. "Measles?"

She shook her head. "Scarlet fever."

Her mother came into the room then with a glass

of water. Maria slid down in her bed and her mother tucked the quilt tighter around her.

I walked along the path with nothing to do. I wondered when I'd have my friend back.

I was full of energy, feet tapping, wanting to climb the cliffs, to fly, to find the cave.

If only I could escape.

SEVENTEEN

MATT

IT was almost September, getting cold. Pop and I had been on the island nearly a year. It was hard to believe. At night now I dreamed of being alone in the kayak, watching birds flying above, listening to the roar of waves as they hit the shore.

During the day as we fished, I tried to think of a way to get past the wires, to the kayak; how lucky I was that no one had seen it yet.

I sneaked away from the house, just before morning, looking. Searching!

There had to be a way out.

I followed the wires, walking around the village, making sure I wasn't spotted by soldiers. The posts were sturdy, the wires looped tight.

It was the dream the next night that made the difference. I saw myself bending the wires, saw them falling away.

I sat up.

The wires had to be joined somewhere. Of course they did. Could I twist them, unwind them? There were pliers in the kitchen drawer, rusty, but I could use them.

I passed Pop's bedroom and stopped. Was he sorry he'd brought me here? He'd said something about it once, turning the page of his book. Afterward, I wondered if he'd really said it, or believed it.

Outside again, the pliers in my pocket, I followed the wires in back of the houses. This time, I felt every one of them slowly, carefully.

I could see through a narrow crack in the wood that the lamp in Maria's room was on. I wondered if she could see me.

I found the knots that held the wires together. It took forever to unwind one of them, even with the pliers doing most of the work. I had to dart away and wait when a soldier walked by. But he didn't leave. He stood there, looking up at the sky.

I'd have to come back again tonight and unwind the rest before I could duck through. I'd put them back together, go out in the kayak, and return before it was light.

*   *   *

That night, I waited until Pop slept. I opened the door a crack and peered outside. The path was empty!

In the darkness, I used the pliers and the wires fell away. I went through and twisted them back, then ran toward the rocks where I'd tied the kayak. I kept looking back, my hands tucked under my armpits. How could I have forgotten my gloves?

I had a quick thought of the end of August at home. Imagine how warm it was!

I reached the cove. Ahead of me the kayak rocked gently on the waves. No one had seen it. At least, I hoped no one had.

Tonight was a problem. It was clear; the moon shone in a path across the water. I'd be visible to anyone who might be searching.

Still, I had to take a chance.

Sliding into the boat, I paddled out of the cove, turning east, watching, worried. A whale breached far out, but that was all.

I knew there was a cove a good distance away where rocks had tumbled into the sea, forming a barrier. I kept going, realizing the moon would actually help. It would be easier to find that inlet.

And there it was, ahead of me. I angled the kayak into the sheltered spot and tied it carefully. Moored there, I hoped it would be hidden from the island and from boats at sea.

I raced back to the house, dodging a soldier on the path, just as Pop was beginning to look for me.

EIGHTEEN

Izzy

ONE morning, I peered into Maria's room, my glasses steaming up against the wood.

A book was open next to her; I could see part of the title: *Myths and Legends*. It made me think of her naming Thor Hill. I wondered if she had named other places. On the bottom of the bed was a basket she'd begun to weave. She'd told me that every basket was different, and after a while, you could tell who the weaver was.

"I'm here, Maria," I whispered, looking back to be sure no one was around to chase me away.

I talked on for a few moments, saying I wanted to know how to weave baskets too, telling her how hungry I was, how I wished I could climb the cliffs and get eggs. "We'd share," I said.

She smiled, nodded. Then she raised her hands,

making twisting motions, thumbs going one way and then another.

What was that about?

"Matt," she whispered.

Her father came along in back of me. "What are you doing here, Izzy? You must let Maria rest." He glanced from me to the hole in the wood and shook his head.

"I'm going home now," I said.

It took the rest of that day for me to guess what Maria had been trying to tell me.

Was I right?

Was she saying that somehow Matt was getting through the wires?

I stayed up that night, watching, half asleep, just about to give up when I saw him coming along the path.

I slid out of bed and opened the door an inch or two. The night was dark, the moon covered by clouds; it was almost impossible to see anything.

Matt walked past. Had he turned, he might have seen me!

Without a sound, I went back for my shoes and reached for my jacket with the hood. Outside, I leaned against the rough wall of the house and shrugged into the jacket. I began to zip it up, but the noise seemed enormous in that quiet night.

Shivering, I left it open.

Even with my eyes used to the darkness, Matt was almost a shadow against the wire fence. He moved slowly and I followed, trying to be as silent as he was.

Where was he going?

The hand on my shoulder was so hard, I almost went down on the ground. Without a word, a soldier turned me around, pushed me back toward the schoolhouse, and pointed to the step in front. I'd seen him before, so unfriendly, marching around the village.

I sat there trembling, the tears coming, my mouth open, the sound of my breathing loud.

What would happen to me?

The dog came and sat next to me, looking for food. I put my arms around him for comfort, leaning against his warm fur.

The soldier never said a word.

He stood in front of me, it seemed for hours, as I listened to the *hoot-hoot* of a snowy owl and cried for Mom. The dark finally lifted, and a pale light came across the island. The fog was thick now, but still I saw the soldier point, mutter something; he waved his arms.

Was he telling me to go?

My legs felt weak; I pressed my hands against the step to help myself stand.

He turned his head, motioning with his chin toward my house. That was all I needed. I was away from there in a moment. I opened my door quickly and went inside.

Leaning against the door, I tried to catch my breath, my hand on my chest.

Mom was still asleep, but she'd be up soon. I couldn't let her know about this night.

I was so tired, though. I threw myself on the couch, then heard the scratch at the door.

I wasn't free after all.

Was the soldier there to take me away? I pulled my woolen hood up, almost covering my head, as if that would save me.

The sound came again; it was whisper soft, but insistent.

But wouldn't the soldier have banged on the door with his fists? I stood and opened it to see Matt standing there, his face like a *williwaw*, stormy and wild. "You will get us killed," he said, his teeth gritted, "following me around like that."

Matt!

I shrugged, closed the door against him, and went back into my bedroom, thinking we weren't killed. And I knew how to get out now.

And that was what I'd do.

NINETEEN

MATT

LATER in the week, I sneaked out and spent time in the kayak. Pulling in, though, I spotted a soldier standing on the bluff overlooking the cove.

I waited endlessly outside the rocks, wondering when he'd leave.

Pop would be waiting, wondering what I was up to.

After a while, I tried again, looking up, searching the cliffs, the beach, even the rocks, which were sprayed with the surf. But he was gone.

A near miss. I shuddered to think of what might have happened had he seen me.

I took a few breaths, made sure the kayak was secure, and hurried back to the house. I closed the door behind me and stopped short. Pop was sitting at the table. What could I say? It was almost worse than being caught by that soldier.

He waved his hand. "I know what you're doing. I've known all along," he said. "We have to talk."

I collapsed onto the seat across the table. I'd hoped for an hour of sleep before I had to fish. Now he was going to lecture me about the kayak, try to keep me from nights in the boat.

I wouldn't listen to him. He couldn't make me, I told myself, even as I knew he could make sure I couldn't go out again.

"I want to tell you . . ." he began, and leaned forward, almost whispering. "I've used the radio for the last time. I've been letting people in the government know what's happening here." He shrugged. "I'll destroy it and drop it into the sea just before we leave."

He went on: "I've heard that we'll be taken off the island, sent to a prison camp on the Japanese mainland. It'll be terrible, not enough food, locked up much tighter than we are here."

I swallowed.

"It'll happen tonight, or early tomorrow morning."

It was hard to believe! We'd spend months, maybe years, in a prison camp far from home. Would Mom even know what had happened to us?

I couldn't let Pop see I was afraid. I lifted my head, kept my mouth still.

"We won't go," he said.

What was he talking about?

"I've hidden a two-man kayak in back of the shed near the harbor. We can do this together. We'll fish, head for another island..."

"It's miles away."

"Better than a prison camp. We'll take a chance."

My throat was so dry, I couldn't answer.

"Listen, Matt. We do have food. We'll bring what we can with us."

I kept shaking my head.

"There's something else," he said.

Were his eyes filling?

"I want to tell you once and for all," he said in his gruff voice. "I've never loved anyone the way I love you. I know I'm irritable. I don't always say the right thing. And I feel worse than I ever did that I brought you here. I wanted you to see how much I cared. And look at the mess I've made."

I looked up at his face, at his eyes, which were brimming with tears. I felt my own tears. *I've never loved anyone the way I love you.*

I took a breath. My voice was as gruff as his when I said, "I love you too." And somehow it was true. What he'd been doing was working secretly for the government. Hadn't I known that all along? Hadn't he given me a chance to be with him? He couldn't have known how terribly this would turn out.

He spread his hands on the table. "So, early tonight you'll go to the kayak and stay there. I'll manage to go to the harbor—" He broke off. "Come back for the food..."

For a moment, he was silent. "I'll bring the two-man kayak to you. The ship will come for the rest of the village, poor people, but we'll be ready to leave."

"How will you know which cove?" I asked. "How will you know where I am?"

"I've been watching you. You're resourceful, brave. I'm proud of you, Matt."

"Why can't we just wait and then come back here to the village?"

"I'm not sure we'll be alone. It's possible that they'll leave men here, or even come back later."

There was no help for it. What could I do? I nodded. "All right."

TWENTY

Izzy

SEPTEMBER! I pulled the beret down over my forehead. I was freezing cold. How soon would we have snow? I couldn't wait.

I walked along the path, hands in my pockets, trying not to trip over stones. I wondered what I'd done with those furry gloves from last Christmas. I still wore my bracelet though. I'd never taken it off.

I thought of my old teacher, Mrs. Dane, maybe because school would have been starting at home. She'd said once, *You could do anything if only you'd set your mind to it, Izzy.* She'd frowned, her forehead a washboard. Was she thinking, *You never do?*

But what she wanted me to set my mind to! Her favorite author, some old guy with a beard to the floor, long division, the history of some place called Mesopotamia, and worst of all, reading every night from the most boring book in the world. *Thirty minutes by the clock,* she'd told the class.

I hadn't done it once.

What made me think of her and that fifth-grade list of miseries?

You could do anything.

The wires were in front of me, twisted together, a rare sun glinting on them. On the other side was the enemy camp, with the soldier from last night staring at me.

I kept walking toward the church, reaching out, one finger on the wires. I stooped, pretending to look at a small yellow flower that grew next to them. Someone had trampled on it.

Then I saw the loop where the wires had been joined together.

I looked up and the soldier was gone.

Could I twist them with my fingers?

Set your mind to it!

I bent down and picked the poor yellow flower with half its petals missing. And glanced up again, looking toward the harbor. Another ship was in the port.

Our army, come to get us?

We'd be free!

But I saw the enemy flag. I turned and went back to the house. Head bent, Mom was working on her book.

I wandered around for the rest of the day, ate the skinny little fish the men brought back, and at last, still hungry, I peered out at the dark.

I waited until Mom slept, until there wasn't a flicker of light from the schoolhouse or the church. I had everything ready: my shoes pointed in the right direction, my jacket zipped so I could pull it over my head.

Outside, I nearly fell over something on the step. I sank down. Wrapped in paper next to me were two small fish.

How had they gotten there?

Matt!

It had to be. He'd been fishing, sorry he'd always been so mean! To make up for it: food!

I stared down at the poor fish; their dead eyes stared up at me. I reached for one.

I was starving!

I ate more than half, tore off a piece of paper to wrap it in, and tucked the other bit in my pocket. Maybe I'd see the dog.

I tiptoed back inside and left the other fish for Mom.

And then I was hurrying, listening for soldiers, watching for them.

I began to twist open the wire loops. It was hard, the wires sharp, and my fingers began to bleed.

Never mind.

One by one, the wires fell away. I ducked through and looped them together again, loosely so I could get back easily.

Strange, no light from the soldiers' camp; I didn't spot one soldier. But tonight, as always, there was fog. It was hard to see far ahead.

The air felt different, maybe because I was free, cleaner maybe, sharp and easier to breathe.

I kept going, vaguely hearing the sound of whistles. I told myself they couldn't be looking for me.

A huge blast came from a ship's horn! Were the soldiers leaving? I couldn't believe it could happen.

I began to climb Thor Hill, stones rattling behind me. I didn't care about noise now; so many sounds were coming from the village.

I stayed out, walking slowly, careful not to slip. I rested on the rocks after a while, thinking about Dad's cave, but I'd never find it on this misty night.

But tomorrow. Or next week. *You could do anything, Izzy.*

I lay on an overhang. A faint glimmer of light was beginning to edge across the sea.

How long had I been free? When would it be dawn? I began to think about going back.

I reached into my pocket for the fish and took another bite. It was salty and good, even raw; I could have eaten a dozen.

The wind began, blowing the fog away. It was a strong wind, a *williwaw*. I caught glimpses of the angry surf.

I squinted at the ship docked close to the landing in the harbor. Was that a line of soldiers climbing onto the ramp? Two of them were dragging a man along. He was fighting them, determined to get free. He wore a jacket that was like Matt's father's. Could that be?

In moments, he disappeared onto the ship.

I leaned over the edge and felt my glasses slip. I reached up, dropping the fish.

But it was too late.

The fish was gone, and the glasses too, so far down, I never heard the sound as they reached the ground.

What was I going to do?

Without my glasses, the whole world was blurred. I'd

always needed them, always put them on the moment I woke, and kept them right next to me in bed at night.

How would I even find my way home?

I blinked, thinking Mom would be awake soon, and she'd know what to do.

I heard another blast of the ship's horn. I squinted at the harbor. Was the ship moving? I couldn't be sure without my glasses, but I thought it might be.

I stumbled down the hill, scattering stones, my hands in front of me, almost like a blind person.

I walked along slowly, grasping the wires then, feeling for the loops, and managed to open them. It was light by the time I reached the village.

How quiet it was. Our door was open, and inside, on the table, was a note. The words were scrawled, not like Mom's usually neat handwriting.

I sat at the table and pulled it toward me. I couldn't see what it said. Not one word. I turned the paper, one way and then another. *Ship. Japan.*

Was Mom on that ship? Was it going to a prison camp? In Japan?

I could hardly breathe.

Was I alone?

Left here, by myself?

—Alone—

Snowy Owl

TWENTY-ONE

MATT

I waited for Pop all night. I kept going over everything
to be sure I'd understood what he'd planned. He'd take
a two-man kayak from the shed, paddle around until he
reached my cove.

How did he know where it was? *I've been watching you.*
Oh, Pop.

I knew now why Mom always stuck up for him. I
thought of that last night at home in Connecticut. What
had Mom said? *You'll see, Matt.*

I'd wondered what she was talking about. I understood now.

Pebbles of sleet stung my head; my hands were cold,
even inside the gloves Pop had made me wear. I could
have wrung the water out of my jacket.

The middle of September on the island, after all.

The kayak swung around, the rope grating against
the rocks. Where was Pop?

I tried to concentrate on his plan again. We'd take the food, fishing rods, and hope for good weather. Would it work?

In the distance, a ship's horn blasted.

I was crying! A big kid, almost as tall as Pop, as good a fisherman as some of the men in the village!

A deserted village.

I slumped over in my seat, eyes closed, soaked with sleet, and waited for Pop.

It was completely light when I climbed up on the rocks looking out. The ship was only a blur on the horizon.

What had happened to Pop?

I went back to the village and threaded my way among the houses, looking for him. The dog barked somewhere.

Maybe I'd see Pop somewhere down near the harbor.

TWENTY-TWO

Izzy

WAS Mom on that ship? I put down the note. I had to get to the harbor. I tried to run, tripped and fell.

Scrambling up, I shouted, "Wait!"

I stumbled over open boxes and suitcases that littered the path in front of the houses, that made me fall again. Everyone must have left in a hurry, probably pushed by the soldiers.

I sank down at the harbor, crying, calling, "Please!"

But the ship was gone.

The sun came up, chasing rain and a *williwaw* away; it glinted on the roofs and the church steeple.

Mom was farther away every minute. She'd be frantic, my soft Mom, wondering where I was, what I was doing. I thought of home. Gram. Even Mrs. Dane. But...

I couldn't stay at the harbor forever. I wiped my swollen eyes with my sleeve and stood up.

What could I do? I could hardly see without my glasses.

The dog was barking. Feeling my way along the path to the church, I went toward him.

I sank down next to him, threw my arms around him, and buried my head in his neck. A bag lay on the church steps, and someone's sweater.

Who'd left them there? And what was in the bag?

I was still hungry in spite of everything. I thought of candy, of lemon cake with icing. I could almost taste a slice of apple pie with vanilla ice cream melting on top.

The dog would be as hungry as I was. What would he dream about? A bone? A biscuit?

I inched forward, reaching for the bag. It was almost empty, a couple of fishhooks, a ball of knotted wire.

I pushed it away from me and put the sweater over my shoulder. I pretended someone was hugging me.

But I had to eat.

I stood up. Maybe something had been left inside one of the houses. A bit of fish, an oyster or two in a pail?

The dog stood next to me. I put my hand on his warm fur to guide me and began to search. It took forever. Maria's house was first. Her bed was rumpled; a blanket lay on the floor. Her books were still there in a pile.

I didn't bother with my own house; I knew there wasn't a scrap to eat.

But Matt's house! On the counter there was food: a box of soda crackers, a bowl of sugar, a few strips of dried salmon, and a tin of flour, dented and old-looking. Maybe Matt's father had brought it from home long ago.

I dipped my fingers into the sugar, sucking up that sweetness. I hadn't tasted anything like it since we'd arrived on the island.

What else?

I chewed on one of the salmon strips and thought again of the dog. I scooped up five or six strips and went back to him.

We sat there eating, my arm around him again. "You belong to me now," I said fiercely. "And I belong to you."

I choked in my breath. I had to stop crying. I had to do something with this day.

I wandered through the village, the dog following, both of us chewing on pieces of salmon. It was so cold, so windy. I glanced up at the blur of mountain. Too late for eggs, of course.

By afternoon, I thought again about the bag with the fishhooks and wire and went back for it. I'd have to give up a little of the salmon, but maybe I'd catch a fish. There might be some berries in the fields. "We'll be all right, I guess," I told the dog. I'd call him Willie, a gray *williwaw*.

Sitting on the wharf, I tried to fish. It took forever to untangle the wire. Without glasses, it was almost impossible to thread the hook on one end and stab a piece of salmon onto it. But somehow I managed.

I dangled the line into the water, but nothing happened. Not even a nibble!

What had I done wrong?

I knew I had to have patience. I watched the horizon, squinting as I searched for a ship, but all I saw was the curve of black water against a gloomy sky.

Hours later, I threw the whole thing onto the sand near the wharf. I'd never be a fisherman.

The sky turned dark. Waves crashed up against the wharf. A tern streaked above me. Mom would have said he was left behind, that he should have been flying toward the sea around the Philippines for the winter.

Left behind like me.

I was glad for the noise of the surf. I didn't want it to be quiet. I wanted to pretend that people were walking back and forth, that Mom was in the house writing in her notebook, or maybe outside, looking up at the birds. I felt an ache in my chest, missing her, wanting her.

I went down to Matt's house and closed the door firmly behind me, shutting out the wind. I ate a little more of the sugar.

It was time to think about what I'd do, here alone. But a ship would come back for me. Mom would tell them.

What if there was no ship for a week? A month?

What if it never came?

Don't think idiotic thoughts, I told myself.

I lit a fire in the stove for warmth, wondering how I didn't burn myself. I thought of the bag of flour, then fell asleep on Matt's couch, to dream of breaded fish, breaded oysters, bread!

I awoke only once during the night, hearing the driving rain on the roof as I pulled a knitted afghan over my feet.

In the distance, Willie barked.

I ate a scoop of sugar on my way outside, but I had to save the rest for later. I left Matt's door open for when the dog came back.

Right now, I needed to go back to my own house and gather warm clothes, and a toothbrush.

From now on, Matt's place would be my place. Somehow the food lined up on the counter made me feel better, made me feel like staying here.

The day was clear. Even though the world was blurred, I could picture dolphins far out, playing in the water.

I heard the sound of engines, and overhead, saw the wings of a plane.

Americans?

It flew low, and as it passed over the island, I stood up on tiptoes, waving.

Of course, the pilot couldn't see me. But there was a pilot. A person. I wasn't so alone. I reminded myself that even in this war, there were people. Someone would find me; I had to hope that.

I went into my house and grabbed everything up that I needed. I stopped to take Mom's sweater too. I'd cuddle around it at night, feeling Mom next to me.

TWENTY-THREE

MATT

I was more than tired after being in the kayak all night, waiting for Dad. When it was light, I finally gave up. I didn't go to our house, though. Not without Pop there.

Instead I went to the schoolhouse, to my old classroom, and lay on the floor, pulling my jacket around me.

I couldn't sleep. I tossed and turned.

What had happened to him?

I went over our plan again and again: the two-man kayak. Pop coming to my cove.

Could I have made a mistake? Or was it something else?

Had he fallen against the rocks somewhere? Or had he been caught by the soldiers and taken to the ship? Maybe he was on his way to a prison camp in Japan.

It was terrible to think about.

I couldn't sleep after all. I'd have to go home, to see if

somehow he might be there. If not, I had to search. And in spite of everything, I was hungry. Would Pop have taken the food, or would it still be in the house?

The door was open. Unlike Pop not to have been more careful. And inside was a mess!

A blanket was balled up on the couch, and the kitchen! A thin line of sugar trailed along the floor. A few strips of dried salmon lay on the table. Pop had said we'd have food. But it had to have been more than this. Someone must have taken some of it.

I glanced into the bedrooms, then went back to the living room and sank down on the couch. Someone had been there, and it hadn't been Pop. Some of the soldiers might have stayed.

The most important thing... I began to tell myself.

What was the most important thing?

To get out of the house.

To get out now.

I raced into my bedroom, grabbed an extra sweater, dry pants, and the jacket Mom had given me before I'd left home, small now, but warm.

I dashed back through the living room and into the kitchen, scooping up salmon, and went out the front door.

I had to find a place to stay while I searched for Pop, and it couldn't be in the village. It had to be where I could see the houses, and maybe the soldiers.

Where?

I couldn't think of that now.

Pop first.

I looked around. Where to begin?

TWENTY-FOUR

Izzy

OUTSIDE, Willie was staring up at me. How hungry that poor dog must be.

I thought of flour, of biscuits. With a pile of stuff in my arms, I went back to Matt's, Willie following.

Inside, I dropped the clothes on the couch and draped Mom's sweater over my shoulders.

I closed my eyes. What had Mom done with flour? She'd swirled it with water, dropped it in a pan.

There was more, but I couldn't remember what it was.

I rummaged around for a pan. Actually, my fingers were doing the finding. How wonderful it had been to see with my glasses.

I pumped water from outside and sloshed it in with the flour. Willie and I watched as my biscuits, if that was what they were, cooked on the hot stone above the fireplace.

"Not too long, I think," I told Willie. "We just have to have a little patience."

Then: "Enough."

I managed to find two plates in the cabinet, scraped out some of the biscuits, which were mostly stuck to the pan, then sat at the table with the dog on the floor next to me.

Willie ate his portion in a moment; it didn't take me much longer, although the whole thing tasted terrible. It filled my stomach, though.

The door flew open.

Matt stood there.

I looked up, shocked. I wasn't alone. I was more than glad to see him!

"You!" he said. "In my house! Eating our food. I should have known."

I was too surprised to answer.

How mean and miserable he was.

But I had messed up his house. Even without glasses, I could see that. Plates filled with burned biscuits, flour on the floor, a pile of my stuff on the bed inside.

Before I could open my mouth, he was yelling!

TWENTY-FIVE

MATT

"YOU'RE a thief, Izzy!" I burst out. I couldn't help it. She had taken the food my father left, spilled almost all the sugar.

She stared at me. No glasses this time. She looked even worse without them: a skinny face, her cheeks red now, pointy nose, and her hair looked like brown strings hanging around her neck, a bracelet looped over her wrist.

"Why don't you and your dog just get out of here," I said furiously.

She was trying to talk at the same time. "I didn't know you were here. I thought I saw your father..."

"That makes it all right to take my stuff?" I stopped. "Where?"

"Going up the ramp to the ship. I thought you'd be there too."

"The ramp?" I felt as if I couldn't breathe.

"He was giving the soldiers a hard time, trying to break loose. It took two of them..."

I opened my mouth, trying to breathe. Pop, on the ship!

Izzy leaned forward. "I thought I was alone."

"You are alone," I managed to say. "I don't want to see you around here anymore. Ever."

"Come on, Willie," she said, nose in the air. She went past me, gathering up a pile of clothes, and stumbled down the steps.

I stood in the doorway and watched her go toward her house, the dog following her.

I had a dog, Merry, at home.

Why was I thinking about my dog? He was safe with Mom.

I was really crying now. I pictured Pop trying to break loose from the soldiers. What must he be thinking? I thought of Mom too. I was glad she didn't know what had happened. Then I wondered. How soon would she find out? Would reporters write about it?

Worse, I was alone, without Mom, without Pop.

TWENTY-SIX

Izzy

I went to my house with Willie, fumbled for the knob, and held the door open for him. "Our place," I said, tears in my voice. "Yours and mine."

I sank down on the couch, the dog at my feet. What could I do next? My feet were tapping, my hands clenched. I couldn't sit still and just listen to the wind whistling around the house.

I went through those small rooms, searching for a morsel of food, searching for anything. I didn't know what. I swept my hands along the bed, along the rickety table beside it. And there was something.

Mom's notebook!

I remembered her earnest face, her voice: *If something happens to me . . . I want to be sure you'll see the birds for me.*

Mom, gone since yesterday.

I touched the pages, almost as if my fingers would

remember her words. But I knew some of them, the list of birds that were rare: the black-tailed gull, the yellow bittern that Dad had drawn, and even some of the plovers. I remembered too the ones she loved that weren't rare: the red-winged blackbirds and the cardinals at home.

I lay on the bed thinking for the first time of my soft bed and the quilt Mom had made for me. Willie jumped up and curled himself around me, his furry tail thumping against my leg. It wasn't night, but I was so sad, so tired and hungry.

There'd be no sugar, no flour for us. "We're on our own," I whispered.

If only I had my glasses.

"That would be a beginning," I said. "Tomorrow, I'll have to climb down the overhang, all the way down, so I can guess the exact spot where they might be."

What if they were broken?

How could they not be broken?

But I had to take a chance. I had to try.

I put my arm around Willie; I was glad to have him there. "I'll never leave you," I said, and closed my eyes to sleep.

* * *

In the morning, I climbed out of bed, remembering I hadn't changed into pajamas last night. I was still wearing the filthy skirt and blouse I'd worn yesterday. Too bad. I didn't care.

"No breakfast," I told Willie. "Glasses!"

I took the endless walk to the overhang with Willie, wondering if I'd recognize it, telling myself that it jutted out farther than any of the other rocky outcrops.

If only I could walk along the edge of the water, squinting up at the exact place where they'd fallen, I'd know where to search below.

My skirt! Filthy, yes, but red, bright red. I could take it off. My coat would cover my slip.

I hung the skirt on the edge of the overhang and anchored it with a rock. Gulls flew high, screeching at me.

I went down the hill, just able to see the path that led to the water. I pulled off my shoes to walk along the sandy shore. It was impossible to see my skirt. Even the overhang was a blur.

Over my shoulder, squinting, I watched waves wash my footprints away. I kept going forward as Willie scampered ahead of me. My mouth went dry. Suppose the glasses had been taken by the sea?

What could I do if I never found them?

Willie was digging under the rocks now, and I stopped to watch. Then he was up, tossing something in the air, eating.

A fish!

I hesitated. *Think!* My fish?

And then I was moving on the sharp grass, watching to see exactly where he was, but he bounded away again.

I glanced up, imagining the skirt waving! And then down at my glasses, one lens cracked!

But mine! A miracle!

I saw the world now: the dark sand under my feet, the spray of the waves, the jagged rocks above, maybe even a whale breaching.

I went back up to get my skirt. I'd get through this. I'd find food for both of us. I'd learn to fish. And someday I'd see an American ship pulling into the harbor, coming for me. "And for you too, Willie. I'll never leave you."

But what I saw instead of a ship was a flock of birds going overhead. Even above the boom of the waves, I heard their cries, almost like bugles. I watched them, dozens of them, gray with gorgeous crimson heads, and then I called Willie. "We have to go home and begin writing in Mom's book."

Later, I flipped through her notes. She'd written: *not rare, but exciting, sandhill cranes, with their wine-colored heads, flying in large groups, crossing the Bering Strait to and from their nesting grounds.*

Maybe they weren't rare, but they were beautiful. I'd add that to Mom's notes in careful handwriting.

TWENTY-SEVEN

MATT

*I*T was cold today; the rain almost looked like sleet. But I thought of the two-man kayak down at the harbor. Maybe I'd take a look. I remembered Pop had planned to use it to meet me. Was it there, waiting for him as he sailed across the Pacific to a prison camp in Japan?

I trudged toward the kayak shed, then leaned back against the wall. I could still see footprints churned up in the mud, three sets, maybe four.

Oh, Pop!

Soldiers must have caught him there, and I could guess how hard he must have fought.

The kayak lay on its side, the sea lion cover ripped and ruined.

I opened the shed door. Kayaks were lined up in a row. Devastation was everywhere! Pieces of wood and scraps of fur were spread across the packed earth.

Not one of them could be used.

Did the soldiers cause all that damage? Or maybe the village people had made sure the enemy couldn't use the boats they'd made so carefully.

Would they ever come back to the island and build new ones?

Outside, the sun had disappeared. Fog had settled over the houses so it seemed that they'd never been there.

I could see only my feet as I walked along the path toward my kayak. I'd still be able to fish in this light; I'd just have to stay close to the shore.

I rushed to the kayak, glad it had been hidden and was safe. I paddled until I came close to a rock that jutted out from the land. Large and gray, it almost seemed like a seal floating in the rough sea. I reached for my fishing line and cast into the waves.

I'd come to love the fog. It made everything mysterious, almost like the shape I saw in the distance. A rock shaped like a seal? A small whale?

I felt a pull on my line and reeled in a fish. I'd captured dinner!

I took a last look at the maybe-seal rock; then I followed the shoreline, which was hardly visible.

I pulled the kayak into its place, tied it up, and went home, carrying the fish.

I thought of eating, thought of Pop, wondering where he was, thought of Mom and how alone she must feel.

TWENTY-EIGHT

Izzy

EVERY day the weather was colder. I picked up pieces of driftwood. Most of the time they were too wet to use, but still I found a few for Willie and me to keep warm. I was lonely for Mom and couldn't stop thinking about Dad. I ate wild celery and found mussels on the beach for Willie and me when I had the energy to take that long walk.

Toward what must have been the end of September, or maybe even the beginning of October, I passed Maria's house, the door swinging back and forth, and went to close it.

I climbed the three steps and I saw a corner of her room: the books on the table, two or three on the floor.

Suppose I read one?

One day I'd tell her I'd borrowed a book. She wouldn't mind. Dad always wanted me to read, and Mrs. Weio had said, *Everyone has to find the right book to fall in love with reading.*

Maybe I'd find one. I didn't think so, though.

I went inside and sank down on the floor. Up close, the books were a mess: covers missing, pages turned down, ripped.

Some of them had *little* in the title: *Little House in the Big Woods*, *Maida's Little Shop;* a bunch had girls' names: Pollyanna, Anne, Rebecca.

I couldn't make up my mind.

Whatever my hand lands on, I told myself. Maybe one with a decent picture on the front.

And there it was: *The Call of the Wild,* with a picture of a dog.

Perfect.

My hand fell on another. I flipped through the pages. There were stories of old legends with pictures.

I remembered the doll punching a hole in the sky, the wind and animals tumbling out.

I tucked the books under my arm.

I went into Maria's kitchen. I knew there was nothing there, but still I searched through drawers, ran my hand over cabinets for crumbs, and gave up at last.

Matt thought I was a thief.

Forget about Matt!

I called for Willie and we went to my house: me to find Mom's notebook, Willie to climb on the bed, fold his thick tail around himself, and take a nap.

I opened the notebook and read all of it. Then I picked up a pencil: *Fall on the island.* I wrote about the wind whipping the surf into froth, and geese, pointed wings the color of waves, snowy white underneath, diving into the water for dinner.

I stood there, imagining food, roast beef with gravy, hot dogs with mustard, and opened the door to see a small fried fish on the step.

Matt, cooking! Trying to make up again.

I chewed on the fish, going past the houses. I'd wait awhile before I told him I was ready to be a friend too. But I really was ready.

The path turned and I walked with it.

Was that a ship anchored close to shore? It wasn't as large as the one that had taken Mom and the villagers away, or even the ship that had brought us here.

Was it American?

I went farther, seeing the curl of smoke coming from a fire near the rocks.

I stopped. Two soldiers were tending the fire;

two others were standing nearby. Behind them was a tent.

They weren't American. They were the enemy!

There was the soldier with the moustache. The others were older and taller.

I lay down on the damp earth and watched, but I didn't see anyone else.

I took a step back, and then I ran!

I reached my house, went inside, and closed the door carefully behind me, locking it. I went into the bedroom and sat on the edge of the bed, rubbing Willie's broad head, trying to calm myself.

I had to be careful. I couldn't wander around the island anymore, not without being sure I wasn't seen.

They didn't know I was here, but what would they do if they found out?

How had all this happened to me!

I couldn't sit there, wanting to hide under the covers. There was one more thing I had to do, and I had to do it now, before I lost my courage, even though the light was fading and it would be night soon.

I had to tell Matt.

—Soldiers—

Yellow Bittern

TWENTY-NINE

Izzy

I pounded on Matt's door until he threw it open. He stood there, glaring at me, hands on his hips. "What?"

"I told you I thought everyone was gone. I thought I was alone."

He raised one shoulder. "So?"

"We're not alone."

He opened the door a little wider. "The Americans have come?"

I shook my head. "At least four enemy soldiers are here."

He pushed at the mop of hair over his forehead; it immediately fell back again. "I guess you can come inside," he said.

"You won't be able to cook anymore. If they smell whatever you're cooking"—I shrugged—"we'll be caught, sent to a camp like our parents."

I hesitated until I was sure I wouldn't cry. "You can't

run around the island. We have to stay hidden. We have to be careful."

"You're imagining things," he said. "There's probably no one here."

I put my hand on the door handle. Too bad. Let him get caught.

"How can I believe a kid like you? Deliberately kicking me on the boat?" he went on. "Ready to push me outside of school. The most unfriendly person . . ."

I couldn't help it. I began to laugh. How could one person think he was so perfect? And he'd gotten most of it wrong anyway.

He turned back to a fish that was simmering in a pan, ignoring me. I took a breath. "Come on, Matt," I said. "I'll show you where they are."

He nodded. "I guess so."

We waited until it was almost dark, not saying a word. At last he asked me if I wanted something to eat.

My mouth watered, but he'd already given me a fish. I opened my mouth to thank him, but he looked so unfriendly, I decided to wait. And I couldn't resist another piece. "I'll just take a little. And a bit for my dog, Willie."

I ate mine fast. I'd never tasted anything so good.

Willie's went into my pocket so I wouldn't be tempted to take a nibble.

It was time! It was cold now and the wind that came from the sea was so strong that we were pushed sideways. It seemed as if it took forever to get there.

Matt grabbed my arm and we stopped, smelling fish frying, hearing clattering, listening to voices.

Behind us there was a sound.

We spun around to see Willie dart past us, barking, going for food. I went toward him and reached for his collar, but I tripped and fell onto the wet sand and Willie kept going.

The soldiers must have heard the dog, and now they'd see him.

I stared at Matt, wiping grit off my face. What would they do to Willie? My poor dog. Why hadn't I made sure the house door was shut?

He was all I had.

THIRTY

MATT

I saw her inch forward. Did she think she could go after the dog?

Was she out of her mind?

I grabbed her arm, but she twisted away from me, crawling just off the path. She was clumsy. I wondered that the soldiers hadn't heard her.

"All I have," I thought she muttered, more to herself than to me.

All I have.

Did I feel sorry for her?

Maybe, but why?

I didn't have anyone either. All I did was fish for food every day.

I followed her, crawling along. My heart was beating so fast and loud I was afraid someone would hear it. I saw smoke rising and then the cooking fire itself. A group of men stood there; one of them held out a piece of fish to the dog. Another patted his head.

They weren't going to hurt him!

"Let it be," I whispered.

She paid no attention. "Come, Willie." Her lips barely moved. The dog looked up toward us, and one of the soldiers took a step away from the fire.

I pulled at her arm; I wasn't going to give up.

At last she crawled back, away from the soldiers, leaving Willie with them.

She left me without saying a word.

It was really late now, or at least I thought it was. At home in Connecticut, the clock would have been ticking in the kitchen.

But not here.

I trudged back to the village. By that time it was entirely dark, and a misty moon shone overhead. I eased my feet out of my shoes and threw myself onto the couch. It was hard to keep my eyes open. I heard myself mumbling: *Food, soldiers.*

And then I slept.

THIRTY-ONE

Izzy

I slid into my pajamas and climbed into bed. I took Mom's notebook with me. Crazy, but it gave me comfort to touch her things. At home, I'd be listening to the radio, *The Lone Ranger* maybe. I swallowed, my throat burning.

Without Willie next to me, it was hard to sleep. I'd just drifted off when I heard noises outside. I sat up, listening.

Someone scratching at the door?

I was afraid to look. Still, I made myself peer through the cracks in the wood covering the windows.

Willie!

I opened the door and he bounded inside, jumping up on me, tongue out, wild with excitement. I sank down on the floor and threw my arms around him, crying, laughing.

He must have eaten his fill, then darted through the circle of soldiers and come home.

To me!

He shook himself and went into the bedroom to climb onto the bed and sleep.

I couldn't sleep, though. I was wide awake. Strange not to know what time it was.

I found Maria's legends book on the chair. I had to find a spot where a light couldn't be seen.

The bedroom had no outside door. No window. I lighted a candle and put it on the floor. Tucking my robe close around me, I leaned against the wall and began to read.

I saw the *williwaw* legend and then opened to a page that began: *In the days before history, two girls fell in love with the moon, but trouble was coming; at least for one of them.*

This wasn't only in a story. It was right here.

How could I escape from the soldiers? Would I ever see Mom again? Or Gram? My teeth began to chatter. Not from cold; I was afraid.

I blew out the candle, left the book on the floor, and went through the living room. I peered out the door, looking toward the village.

Smoke rose from one of the houses, and a light flickered in the darkness!

Matt!

He was going to get himself captured, and me with him. *Trouble.*

It was a distance to the enemy camp, but maybe the soldiers would search to be sure no one else was on the island.

I pulled on my coat over my pajamas and tiptoed outside, remembering to close the door. Barefoot, I walked along the edge of the path.

I banged on his door. Never mind quiet. It was too late for that.

He threw open the door. "Now what?"

I pushed him inside. Almost. He was much bigger and stronger than I was.

"I knew it." He slammed the door behind us. "Something is wrong with you."

"Light, smoke," I answered furiously. "Something is wrong with *you!*"

He looked around. I could tell he was embarrassed. "I didn't think anyone could see."

"Wrong." I bit my lip before I could say *again.*

He blew out the candle and the room grew dim. "I

have oysters," he said. "I was saving them for the morning, but if you want some..."

"No."

He shrugged.

I waited a moment to calm down. "There's a cave," I told him. "My father said so. If we found it, we could move everything in there. Maybe we could even have light. We might be safe."

He didn't say anything for a moment. "I think Pop said something about a cave. I can't remember exactly..."

I took a chance. "Want to look for it with me?"

I waited for him to answer.

He shrugged again. "I guess so. Tomorrow."

"It may be a forever search, I'm warning you."

"You think I can't do that?" He closed his mouth. I could see how angry he was.

THIRTY-TWO

Izzy

WE had to find that cave. I stopped. What had Dad said about it? So many things!

I tried to remember: there was nothing about how big it was, nothing about where it was on the island. It was hard to think. I was so hungry.

Wait!

Once when we talked about the island, he'd said, "I looked down. I could see the ocean stretching out forever."

The ocean, not the sea.

So, the Pacific Ocean; the south side of the island.

And Mrs. Weio: *two rocks bowing to each other when it's calm.*

It was still early. While I waited for Matt, I read another page of the legends book. The moon would choose only one of the two girls.

But now, Willie was at the door. He was hungry too. Did he want to go to the soldiers?

I hesitated, but he needed to eat. I was careful to open the door slowly, peering along the path to be sure the soldiers weren't nearby.

Willie darted out but looked back almost as if he wanted me to come with him.

If only I could! I hadn't had enough to eat for days.

"Go, Willie," I whispered, and closed the door carefully. I leaned against it, worrying suddenly that he'd lead the soldiers back here, back to me.

What could I do? I couldn't sit still anymore. I rubbed my hands against my skirt. Mom's bird book was on the counter and I paged through it, seeing descriptions of birds I'd never heard of, the horned puffin, and the king eider with its orange bill. I wondered about Dad's yellow bittern. Would I ever see it? Imagine how happy that would have made him.

Matt was knocking at the door. I grabbed the notebook and put a pencil behind my ear, in case I saw interesting birds.

Outside, we took the long path away from the

soldiers. "The cave," I said. "We have to search along the Pacific side."

Hours later, we saw the ocean. We began to climb, crossing diagonally, searching for an opening in the rocks. From high up, the water looked almost like a mirror. I saw ships, almost as if they were painted on that glass.

Ships! More soldiers?

I glanced over my shoulder. Matt was looking out at the ocean too. What was he thinking? Maybe he wished he were out there on the water.

I reached the highest rock, turning slowly. I tried to see an opening, no matter how small. I glanced down, checking the paths below to be sure we were alone.

A bird with yellow wings flew over my head and swooped down to teeter on a ledge nearby. I hardly moved, hardly breathed. But Matt called and the bird took one or two tiny running steps and flew.

That was it. Not only had he ruined my view of the bird, he was loud enough to be heard by anyone nearby.

"You're an idiot," I said.

He stepped back, surprised. Then his arms churned . . .

He tumbled over the rocks and disappeared below. I couldn't imagine that he wasn't badly hurt.

I followed him, holding on to rocks. I tripped, bruising my elbow. But never mind. I had to get to him.

Had that miserable boy killed himself?

"Please no," I heard myself saying.

THIRTY-THREE

MATT

I rolled down the hill, stones cutting my back, my arms, my legs. I hit my head and kept falling. The world was dizzying: black rocks and gray sand, one above the other, turning in a perfect circle.

The ocean roared in my ears. Would I hit the water and be carried far out?

But with a wrench to my knee, and to my elbow, I stopped. I closed my eyes.

Dreaming. Pop was yelling, Izzy was yelling *No!* Angry... I yelled too. *I'm not going to the islands with you, Pop. Mom, I'm hurt.*

I opened my eyes to mist, to fog, to Izzy bending over me, her glasses halfway down her nose.

What was she crying about? Saying "No," over and over? What was I doing there anyway? Lying on the ground, a stone under my shoulder?

"Matt?" Izzy was whispering. "Are you alive?"

Of course I was alive. She couldn't even see that? "Your glasses are a mess," I said.

She really was crying.

"What are you doing here?"

"Helping you," she answered. "What do you think?"

"Who knows?" I looked past her, high up to the top of the hill. I remembered then, I had fallen.

I sat up. "All right. I'm..." I stopped. My knee was through my pants, bloody, and when I moved, it didn't want to move with me. I tried to close my mouth over the groaning noise I was making, but I couldn't stop.

But Izzy wasn't looking at me. She was staring down at the water, at a pair of rocks. She pushed at her glasses. "Don't move. Stay there. Just give me a few minutes. I'll be back."

I really didn't want her to go. Strange. But moving was a problem. I watched her scramble back up the hill, hand over hand on the rocks.

Would she leave me there?

It was too much to think about.

I closed my eyes again.

THIRTY-FOUR

Izzy

I was still trembling, thinking about Matt sprawled out against the rocks.

I told myself to stop. He was alive; he was breathing. But his knee. Oh, his knee.

How could I help him? There was something . . .

What had I seen in the water?

Two rocks, bowing.

Then, maybe, the cave could be above us.

I left Mom's notebook just off the path, the pages fluttering. No time to bother with it, as precious as it was. I kept going, climbing the rocks again, looking for an opening.

And there it was.

Ducking my head, I peered into the cave, reaching out to touch the rocks at the entrance. My father might have done that long ago. And on a sunny day I might have brought Mom here to look for birds flying overhead.

I took a step inside and looked back. Far along the path below, a few soldiers were marching. The ships! More of the enemy! These were not the same soldiers as the ones I'd seen near the harbor.

They'd be on top of Matt in minutes.

Hands grasping the rocks, I slid down to him.

"We have to move," I said.

"I don't think..." he began.

I didn't let him finish. "They're coming. The soldiers. We have no time. We have to do this."

I put my hands under his arms and tried to lift him. How heavy he was!

Mrs. Dane: *You could do anything, Izzy, if only you set your mind to it.*

I took a breath, helping him sit up. One knee was so full of blood, I had to look away. He leaned against me and managed to stand, but bent over like the old grandmother from the village.

We began to climb, but so slowly, I couldn't imagine that the soldiers wouldn't be directly underneath us in seconds.

I held on to Matt, bearing his weight, saying it over and over in my mind: *You could do anything, Izzy... anything.*

Somehow we reached the cave. I helped him sit close to the entrance; it was as far as he could go. We sat on the hard stone floor, blinking in the dim light.

And then I remembered. Mom's notebook. On the ground, just off the path.

Where were the soldiers now? Had they seen it?

I looked over Matt's shoulder.

They were still on the path, but marching away.

I raised myself higher. "Safe," I whispered, hardly able to speak.

I sat there, trying to calm myself. As soon as I could, I wanted to walk farther in, to see how far the cave went. But first the notebook!

Please let it still be there.

I clambered down the side of the rocks, tearing the hem of my coat. But it was there, damp now, some of the pages curled, some bent.

But still, the soldiers hadn't seen it! I scooped it up and climbed back inside. "Going to explore," I told Matt, who didn't answer.

The cave was deeper than I'd thought. I held on to one side, moving slowly, until ahead of me was a trickle of water.

In front of me, a fountain streamed down into a

narrow pool. I sank down on the cave floor, held my hair back, put my face into the icy water, and drank. The sound of my gulping was loud in this place surrounded by stones.

I stood and took another few steps, following a turn in the cave. Light and a misty fog came from an opening in the back of the cave.

Far below were tents.

Too many tents to count.

There must have been hundreds of soldiers there!

No place was safe!

Not us.

Certainly not us.

THIRTY-FIVE

MATT

"WATER," Izzy said, cupping a torn piece of her skirt in her hands. Water dripped along the rocks.

I'd never been so thirsty. But instead of putting it to my mouth, she washed the blood away from my knee. "It's twice the size it should be," she said.

I didn't care about the blood. I just wanted to take that cloth and suck on it, washing away the terrible dryness in my mouth.

I wouldn't ask her.

But she was gone again, moving toward the back of the cave, and came back moments later with the cloth. Washed of blood, it dripped cool water into my mouth.

She never stopped talking, telling me about the fountain and the soldiers' camp below. "There are too many tents to count."

She took a breath and began again. "You won't be

able to go back to the village with that knee the way it is. But don't worry, I'll find food."

She pushed her hair away from her face. "Blankets. Cups. Bandages." She narrowed her eyes. "I'll steal whatever I have to."

I turned away from her. The pain in my knee was much worse now. It was hard to think about anything else.

She was right. The village was miles away. I wouldn't even be able to climb down the side of the cliff.

I thought of the terrible climb we'd taken a little while ago. How had she carried most of my weight? It was hard to believe: a skinny thing like her.

I was stuck with her now, almost as much a prisoner as Pop was, so far away, I thought irritably. Then, *Mean*, I told myself.

Izzy slept at last, breaking off midsentence about learning how to dig for clams.

I couldn't sleep. I tried to stand.

Tried.

Tried again.

Then, leaning against the wall, I managed to inch my way along the cave.

A thin stream of sand was coming from openings

where the rocks were not quite seamed together. Were we safe here?

It took forever to get to the fountain and that small pool. And that was as far as I could go.

I lowered myself down, sitting with my back against the wet wall. I looked at my shoes. There was no way to get them off.

I inched into the water, which just covered my knees. Never mind the shoes.

It was freezing, but it numbed my knee, washing the rest of the blood away.

Long ago, it seemed, I was in Connecticut. Maybe today I'd be at the Y with Mom, watching her swim, timing her. I closed my eyes. Years ago when I had mumps, she'd sat on the couch with me, reading aloud.

If only I could see her for just five minutes.

How had this happened to me?

Did I feel sorry for myself?

I did. And why not!

THIRTY-SIX

Izzy

I awoke in the dark, aching from lying on the hard stone floor, my teeth chattering from the cold. Where was Willie, I wondered.

I glanced across at Matt. He was awake and I could see from his face how much pain he was in. How long would it take him to heal? We had to leave here before we were caught. There were so many soldiers; we couldn't hide from them for long.

Still, I had to bring things back from the village, otherwise we'd freeze. But the soldiers! I couldn't wait for daytime; I had to go now in the dark.

It would take all night. Could I leave Matt for that long? Could I walk across the island without being seen?

I stood up quickly. I had to stop scaring myself.

I leaned over him. "I'm going to the village."

He nodded, then held up his hand. "Wait, Izzy. I just thought of something. My father had a radio hidden under the floorboards. I'm sure he broke it up, but maybe there wasn't time. Maybe it's still there." Matt grabbed my arm. "I can't believe I didn't think of it sooner. It's probably gone, but just maybe..."

His voice trailed off. His leg was bleeding again. Through his torn sleeve I could see that his elbow was raw. I had to get bandages.

At the mouth of the cave, I peered down at the path. It was empty. I climbed out and down the rocks, looking over my shoulder.

If they came, would I have time to hide? I hurried, making my way in the foggy darkness, walking all those miles. Stopping to rest, I wondered why those soldiers were there, feeling an ache of homesickness.

When I finally reached the village, I went from house to house: the village chief's first, even though I'd been there once. The old grandmother's was next. A bit of stale bread, but nothing else.

I found a piece of salmon in the last house. Outside, I gave half to Willie. But I couldn't wait another minute to go to Matt's house, all the while thinking, *Floorboards, maybe a radio. Saved.* We'd have help.

By this time, it was light, almost morning. I heard the sound of a cuckoo, but he was too sneaky to be seen.

Like me, I hoped. I'd add that to Mom's notes when I had time.

Inside Matt's house, I leaned against the wall.

Why floorboards? Did we even have floorboards in my house? It seemed to me the floor was nothing but packed earth.

And where? In what room?

"If I wanted to hide something under the floor," I said aloud, "it would be..."

Under the table? No. Someone might see where the floor had been torn up.

So, out of sight. I went into the bedroom and looked down. The boards were wide, uneven. I pushed the bed hard until it began to move, an inch, then more.

I ran my hands over the floor and caught a huge splinter in my finger.

But nothing was there.

I pulled at the splinter, which didn't want to come out, as I went into the other bedroom and pushed that bed aside.

I crawled across the dusty floor, and yes, feeling with my fingers, I could tell the thick boards were not quite fitted together.

A radio. Please.

I pried up the boards, three, then four, and one more. There was no radio.

Oh! I sat back. Willie leaned over my shoulder. I was looking down at a treasure of food!

I ran my hands over boxes wrapped in waxed paper. It was hard to believe. More flour, sugar, dozens of strips of dried salmon, oats, raisins. I thought of Gram. Sometimes I'd stay at her house. She always made oatmeal with a raisin face.

I sat back on my knees for a second, yanking at the splinter, which finally came free. I couldn't wait to get back to the cave with all of this. It would keep us alive!

Then I realized. We weren't saved. We'd still have to help ourselves. And I had to find bandages. Nothing was more important.

My house, maybe. And on the front step was a pail of mussels in seawater. Matt was such a strange boy. One minute he was nasty, the next doing something that made a difference. When had he left them? Why hadn't I seen them?

I took the pail inside with me and pulled blankets off the bed, took Mom's winter robe and even a pillow. In the bathroom, I saw the legends book. I had to see which girl the moon chose. And *The Call of the Wild!*

But bandages. There were none in the house, none in the whole village. Only filthy towels, rags crusted with mud.

I felt a pain in my chest. I went back into my bedroom and stood there, looking at the pink party dress. I ran my hand over its softness. For the hundredth time I thought of Gram, pictured her sewing the velvet buttons. Would I ever see her again?

Dear Gram. I'd have to give up the dress.

I slid it off the hanger, feeling tears on my cheeks. Ripped into long pieces, it would make fine bandages.

I shook myself. I had to hurry. I couldn't carry everything back. I'd have to make another trip, at least one, maybe more.

All right, what then?

Enough food for a few days, especially the oats.

I couldn't forget the mussels at my house, a knife to open them. A cup, two bowls.

The dress.

We had to have something warm. I'd wear Matt's coat and his dad's over that. I'd put food in my suitcase and carry the blanket and my dress around my shoulders like a cape.

But that was all. Even that much would slow me down for the miles I'd have to walk without being seen.

As I left the village, Willie bounded back and forth, waiting for me to catch up.

When we turned to climb the rocks at last, dragging the blanket, I felt drops on my head. Rain? Maybe snow. But it was something in between. Sleet!

Matt was propped up against the wall, his shoes wet. "The radio?" he asked.

I shook my head, then dropped the blanket and opened the suitcase to show him the food. "Under the floorboards," I said.

He spoke slowly, thinking it through. "Pop said we had food. I thought it was the sugar and the flour I'd seen that first night."

I shrugged out of his dad's coat, and then his.

He nodded, and for once, smiled. "Thanks. Hungry."

"Yes, me too."

I sank down next to him. "We'll have our own Thanksgiving dinner," I told him. But even as I said it, I was afraid. Soldiers were almost on top of us. How long could we stay here?

Matt looked up at the rocky ceiling, frowning. "I think Thanksgiving must be past." He smiled again.

I smiled back: a moment of peace between the two of us. But then I sat there, tearing the dress I'd loved into bandages, trying not to cry. I wrapped the pieces around his leg and his elbow.

"Pink?" he said, not sounding happy.

I couldn't believe it! I stamped back to the fountain and filled the cup. We'd have to share.

Back at the blanket, I opened mussels on the cave floor.

He opened his mouth to say something, but I glared at him. "Open your mouth, and I'll leave here."

We ate without speaking, Willie nosing into my arm. I gave him one of the slippery pieces. Why not? We had enough to last us for a while.

Matt was moving around now, trying to stand. "I can't stay in here forever!" he burst out.

I sighed. Impossible as he was, I had to feel sorry for him. "Give it a few days. A few weeks."

"And what will I do in the meantime?"

"Listen to me. I'll read an old legend about a girl who married the moon."

He sighed. "I guess."

And so I began. "*Each girl wanted the moon to choose her. But the moon would marry only the patient one. He* grabbed them by the hair and rushed them high up toward the place where he lived..."

I thought about patience. Matt didn't have any.

But did I?

Slow down, Mrs. Dane always said.

Never mind. I'd spend a little time writing about birds flying overhead, about the clouds scudding across the sky. I'd try not to think about what I'd be doing at home.

THIRTY-SEVEN

MATT

IZZY was gone again the next night, bringing back more of Pop's food.

She mixed oats with water, and we sat eating. Afterward, I asked her to take off my shoes. I hated to do it, but they were wet and stiff and were almost as bad as the pain in my knee.

She worked at the knots in the laces while I tried to stay still.

For the first time, I understood why she was always tapping her hands and feet.

I thought she'd never get them off. But she did, finally, and peeled my socks off too.

Not a great job for her.

"Thanks," I said.

She waved her hand but didn't answer.

I leaned against the wall, thinking I had to heal. I had to be able to walk soon. Not only were the soldiers a worry. But there was something just as fearful. Sand drifted from the cave ceiling all the time.

It was a strange morning. I didn't hear the *hiss-boom* of the surf far below. And the light was odd, much darker than usual.

"Look." Izzy stood at the mouth of the cave. "It's snowing!"

Thick flakes were coming down, and in moments we couldn't see the ocean, or even the rocks. Snow drifted in and piled up inside, several inches deep.

She grinned at me. "It's blocking the wind. It's warmer now."

"We won't have to worry about soldiers today," I said slowly. "No one will be moving. Not even Willie."

But next to me was a tiny pile of fine gray sand, and as I looked up it seemed as if one of the rocks had shifted. *Please hold,* I thought. *At least another few days. Weeks?*

The next morning the snow tapered off. And later, a blinding sun pierced its way into the cave.

We peered outside. The path was hidden under inches of snow; the snowy rocks, just soft pillows now, glinted in the light.

"We have food," Izzy said. "We have the legends

book, and Mom's bird book to look at. We'll be all right, Matt."

I wasn't so sure. I tried not to listen to the faint sting-ing sound of the sand against the rocks as Izzy began to read aloud: *"The moon dropped one of the girls through the sky because she had lost patience. The other, his new wife, was fascinated with one-eyed people. 'Stars,' he told her."*

Izzy tapped the book. Not surprising. She was always tapping something. "Imagine," she said, "thinking that stars were people."

When was the last time I'd seen stars? In the Sound? Or maybe from my bedroom window in Connecticut. I tried to bend my knee. If only I could get into my kayak, away from here.

But then what about Izzy? There was room for only one in the boat.

I'd have to figure all that out. Somehow. I knew, though, we had to be ready to leave soon.

I looked out; a few fine flakes were coming down again.

It almost seemed as if we might be buried here.

THIRTY-EIGHT

Izzy

FOR the next week or so, I kept looking out at the snow, thinking of Christmas in Connecticut. It had to be close to that time.

Mom would attach pieces of bread to the wash line with clothespins for the winter birds. And Gram would be fixing a feast in the kitchen, feeding me bits of sugary apples for the pie, telling me about her favorite of Dad's books. I wished I could think of the title, but all I remembered were the presents piled under the tree in the living room.

Mom and Dad not here! No Gram! And everything we ate was cold. I pictured the turkey! Mashed potatoes! Leftovers! Was I ready to cry again?

The weeks passed. I tried to keep track of the time. But everything was the same: snow coming down, the wind hurling sleet into the mouth of the cave; our food supply, which had been huge, was beginning to dwindle.

I kept myself busy writing in Mom's book: birds like arrows darting across the pewter sky, snow spattering on the curl of waves. And early mornings, I'd sit at the edge of the cave for light, waiting for Matt to wake. I'd finished the book on legends and begun *The Call of the Wild*.

That was us, Matt and me, in the wild with Willie.

"How long do you think we've been here?" I asked Matt early one morning.

His voice was bitter. "Forever."

"If only we had hamburgers and French fries," I said.

Matt stared at me.

For a moment, I thought he looked sad.

"With onions," I said.

He hobbled toward the back of the cave. "I hate onions," he said, and then, under his breath, "I have to get out of here. I can't stand it anymore."

He was stronger now. I could see that he was almost ready to leave.

But we couldn't leave.

I had watched the soldiers on the other side of the cave building fortifications, shouting back and forth. So many of them. But the snow on the path in front of us was almost smooth. And even though there were bare patches on the rocks we could use to climb down, our footprints would stand out and give us away.

At last, the snow tapered off. Could it be February? March? Mrs. Dane always had us write the date carefully on every piece of work we did for her.

The sleet turned to a steady rain. Birds I'd never seen, or hadn't spotted since last fall, were flying toward the island.

I watched sandpipers, those speckled birds with long beaks that Mom loved. Hundreds ran along the shoreline on legs like pipestems with tiny clawed feet.

One afternoon, when a pale sun like a lemon drop appeared, Matt said, "Just a few more days, then I'm going to get the kayak." He hesitated. "There's only room for one."

I raised my hand in the air, an I-don't-care wave. "Go ahead," I said, swallowing hard.

−1943−

Peregrine Falcon

THIRTY-NINE

Izzy

I was dreaming of Dad, taking pictures of things he loved. Gram was in the dream too. "You're my best girl," she said. "And your mother..."

Matt shook me awake. If he had just waited another minute I'd have had more of that dream. "It's morning. I'm leaving. Now. You'd better get out too."

What was he talking about?

He almost pulled me toward the back of the cave. "We can't come back, Izzy. Look up."

For the first time, I saw it. A thin stream of sand or tiny pieces of rock was spilling onto the floor of the cave.

I stood there, trembling a little. "Do you think the cave will collapse?"

He shrugged. "I told you. We have to get out, get away from the cave, away from soldiers."

Dad's cave! I'd looked for it all this time, and now it would be gone. It was just too much.

"Aren't you sick of it here anyway?" he asked.

I nodded. Still, I was crying as we gathered everything that was left: the blanket, the food, clothes. I put the velvet buttons in my pocket. Maybe someday Gram would make me another dress and sew on those beautiful buttons.

"I'll try for my kayak," he said, shrugging into his coat.

He'd take the kayak, and I . . .

What would I do?

Don't think about it now!

Holding on to the rocks, we navigated the packed snow as quickly as we could. We watched, though, both of us. It would be hard to hear the sound of soldiers' boots above the crash of the waves.

I watched Willie too. Maybe he'd bark if he saw soldiers.

Hours later, tired, we reached the path that led to the sea. Matt went ahead of me and turned off.

It was easy to see he didn't think I was going with him. After all these weeks! Months! He would just leave me here, alone.

"Hey!" I called. "What about this stuff? Don't you want some of the food?"

"Leave it all there," he answered. "I'm just going out for a while to see what the sea is like. I'll be back."

Before he could see how relieved I was, I turned away, watching Willie, who was chasing clumps of snow. I held my head up, as if I didn't care what Matt did or where he went.

I wondered if the four soldiers were still in the village, or if they'd gone to join the others in the south.

I was too tired to walk one more inch, so I sank down on a rock, with Willie next to me. I looked back, still searching for soldiers.

Over my head, a bird swooped down and grabbed something. A smaller bird maybe, poor thing. How fast that bird moved! Another bird I could say I'd seen. It was a peregrine falcon. I recognized his trim brown body, his tremendous speed, from Mom's book.

I looked down toward the sea. Matt was there. He raised his arms, then lowered them.

"Matt?"

He didn't hear me. Of course not. He was only a few feet from the surf.

I walked toward him. "Matt," I said again as I went closer.

Still he didn't turn.

I was right behind him, my hand out, when he saw me. "What do you want?" he asked.

He was crying.

"What is it?" I yelled so he could hear me over the boom of the surf.

"Nothing."

How strange to see his tears, this tough kid.

I shaded my eyes against the light to see. The kayak had drifted away. One moment it was visible on the crest of a wave, the next, it disappeared until the swell rose again.

I reached up and put my hand on his shoulder.

I thought he'd push my hand away, but he didn't. "The rope was tangled somehow," he said. "I tried to loosen it, but it slid into the sea, and the kayak..."

I knew the rest. He'd lost the only thing on the island he cared for.

As long as we were there, he'd never get out on the water again.

FORTY

MATT

WHAT would we do now? Where would we go?

"It's almost dark," Izzy said. "Let's sneak back into the village as soon as the light is gone and spend the night at one of the houses. Then tomorrow..." She raised her shoulders in the air. "Who knows?"

And that was what we did. My knee was aching, and I needed to sleep.

We stayed in the house closest to the end of the village: Mrs. Weio's house, with books and papers stacked on the couch.

This was a good place, I thought. We could rush out the back door and be gone if we saw soldiers coming toward us.

Maybe.

"Take the bed," I told Izzy.

For once, she nodded. At least I thought she did.

I ate a handful of raisins, standing at the kitchen table, then I lay on the floor and closed my eyes.

I dreamed of the Sound, dreamed of the gentle waves, dreamed of rowing. I saw Mom's smiling face as she watched me.

In one moment, it seemed, Izzy was leaning over me, shaking my arm.

"Go away," I said. "It isn't even morning."

"It's just light and I heard a bird, somewhere in the village. Its song is the most beautiful I've ever heard. I'm going out to look. Maybe I'll be able to see what it is."

She was gone before I could say anything, before I could warn her to be careful.

I thought of going after her, but I had to close my eyes for a second.

And then I slept.

FORTY-ONE

Izzy

JUST past the end of the village, I caught a glimpse of the bird, mostly brown, not really pretty. But oh, that song.

Then I realized. Starred in Mom's notebook: a Eurasian skylark.

I stood there, entirely still, listening, as it perched on a bit of grass.

The song stopped and the lark startled up.

Everything around me was still.

Too still.

Then, footsteps?

Willie came bounding up and stood in front of me. Had he heard the steps too?

Someone was coming toward us.

I dropped to the wet ground, grabbed Willie's collar, and pulled him down with me. Mud covered my cheek, the side of my neck; it oozed up between my fingers.

We lay there forever, it seemed. I was wet and chilled through.

The footsteps were silent now.

Was he listening?

It was as if he could hear Willie's breath, or my teeth chattering and my heart thrumming up into my throat.

Why hadn't I been more careful?

If only the fog would roll in, covering us like a blanket, hiding us.

Feet pushed loose branches aside.

He was yards away, then...

I moved my head the slightest bit. I had to see.

A stone's throw away, he stared down at us.

FORTY-TWO

MATT

*I*ZZY was back, leaning against the door, looking even worse than usual.

For a moment she was quiet. "Something happened just now," she said at last. "Outside the village. I was caught by a soldier."

I wanted to say, *Why weren't you more careful?* But hadn't I known we'd be caught sooner or later?

"I heard his footsteps, and there was no place to go," she went on. "Nowhere to hide. He was right there in front of us, hands on his hips, chewing on his moustache."

I raised one hand. "He's coming here, then, coming for us."

"Just listen, Matt. The soldier reached out and touched Willie's head. 'I am being sent south, others will stay for a short time,' he told me. 'Within weeks, there will be battles. You must prepare to go, to find a place to hide.' When he turned to walk away, he said, 'I hope you found the fish and the mussels.'

"On my doorstep," Izzy said. "I thought it was you, Matt." She went on. "At first, I was too shocked to answer. I know I'd begun to cry. But then I called after him. 'Thank you. I hope you get home safely.'"

Izzy and I didn't speak for a long time. There was too much to think about. The soldier had known we were on the island all this time.

The enemy.

Things aren't always the way you think they are, Pop had said.

The Americans were coming.

But where could we go?

Where could we hide from their bombs until the battle was over?

FORTY-THREE

MATT

IT was just light when Izzy said, "I have an idea, something we could do."

She leaned forward. "I was thinking about the other kayaks. The ones that belonged to the fishermen."

"Ruined," I said. "All of them."

"We'll fix—"

I cut her off again. "The frames are smashed. The coverings are torn."

She frowned. "My old teacher said you can do anything if you set your mind to it."

I shook my head. "You'll see."

"Good, let's go."

I sighed, a loud sound, to let her know I thought it was ridiculous to bother.

She sighed right back, rolling her eyes as if I were an idiot.

We circled the village, looking for soldiers, but the

path was clear. At the harbor, I pulled open the shed door and closed it behind us, except for a few inches so we could see.

Izzy walked back and forth, stepping over pieces of wood, bones, and shreds of sea lion skin.

"You could do anything, Izzy," she was muttering, "if only you'd set your mind to it." She looked over her shoulder at me. "A big guy like you giving up without even trying?"

Hands on her hips, she tapped her feet against the packed-earth floor. Her glasses were cracked, her hair stringy; she was a mess. She bumped into the fishing gear propped up in the back corner.

But I thought of what she'd done: she'd half-carried me up the mountain, brought me water. She'd gone to the village more than once to bring back food and things to keep us warm.

So maybe she was right about trying to fix a kayak.

It was our only hope... until, maybe, the Americans came.

"Izzy the Mosquito," I said, but I said it nicely.

She smiled. "A mosquito that stings," she said. "So now, let's find the kayak that's the least damaged and work on that."

We spent the morning picking over each one. Some were too big, impossible for me to paddle alone. Three could never be repaired.

But...

There was one with two seats, upright, leaning against the back of the shed!

I could teach Izzy. We couldn't make a long trip the way Pop had planned, but yes, we might make the far end of the island, away from the battle.

I pointed at the kayak. "This one."

Before I could say another word, she was pulling kayaks out of the way, and I rushed to help her drag the two-seated one to the center of the space.

We stood there, staring at it. Whoever had ruined the others had almost missed this one. The frame seemed fine; it was only the covering that was damaged.

I pointed to it. "Here's the problem," I said. "We could never—"

"Mrs. Dane would have a problem with *you*," Izzy said.

I didn't ask who Mrs. Dane was. I could guess.

Izzy was squinting at the skin. "If I had a

needle, curved, large, and some kind of thread, waxed maybe..."

"Maybe you could steal that stuff from a fisherman's house," I said, but I grinned at her.

She held up her hand. "Listen," she whispered.

We could hear the soldiers' voices as they came close, and we saw a hand begin to push the heavy shed door farther open.

We didn't stop to think. Izzy slid under one kayak, and I slid under another.

I didn't breathe.

I wondered if they could hear my heart pounding. It seemed to be up somewhere in my throat.

From where I was, I could see a patch of light on the floor next to me and boots covered with mud. The soldiers were speaking, but I had no idea of what they were saying.

Then they were gone, leaving the door open behind them. We waited, whispering to each other after a few minutes, from one kayak to the other, not sure how close they were.

I couldn't stand it anymore. I slid out from underneath and, still on my hands and knees, went to the door.

They were at the harbor. They'd have to pass here on the way back.

We waited.

An hour? Two?

Then at last they walked past and I could breathe again!

FORTY-FOUR

Izzy

WE were more than cautious, moving only at night, peering around the corners of the houses, standing still until we were sure we were alone. We could only be certain that one soldier was friendly.

It was hard to find what we needed to sew the kayak; most of the time it was too dark to see, until one night, there was a dusty moon. I could see!

I found a long curved needle in the grandmother's house, and then waxed seal thread still hanging on a line in back of one of the fishermen's houses.

I remembered Mrs. Rizzo's sewing class in my old school. What a torture that had been!

But I could sew, slowly and awkwardly, maybe the way I read, but bit by bit, a little at a time, when I thought we were safe. I managed to attach the sea lion skin to the top of the kayak's frame.

And Matt? Fishing from the shore, to get whatever he could for us to eat. My mouth watered, thinking of fluke or flounder.

Imagine. At home I wouldn't even touch a piece of fish.

Every night he baited the hook with a small piece of salmon, and sometimes he brought in a small fish. Not much more than a bite each. But even so, it was something. Our old food supply had dwindled to almost nothing.

At last the kayak seemed ready. He began to teach me to paddle. He had almost no patience. "Not like that, Izzy," he'd say, sitting behind me in the kayak. He'd move his hands, showing me. "Faster," he'd say, or, "Slower."

I felt as if I'd burst. "Do you have to complain every minute? Do you enjoy being so irritable?"

"I just want..." he began. "I can't help..." His hand went to his mouth. "You think I'm irritable?"

"Are you kidding?"

He turned away from me. "Oh, Pop," I thought he whispered. Were there tears in his voice?

One night, we managed to move the kayak from the

shed, carrying it over our heads, taking a huge chance that we'd be caught. It took forever, moving slowly, trying not to make a sound.

He chose a cove that was sheltered, and maybe, fingers crossed, a place that the soldiers didn't bother with.

"This time," Matt said, "we'll be careful of the rope." He sounded almost as if I'd been the one to lose his boat.

It was time to try the kayak in the water, for me to sit in one of the cockpits and paddle.

"You know how, I think," Matt said, almost gritting his teeth.

But I didn't. It was a disaster. But we kept working at it, Matt muttering, "One. Two. Right. Left. Terrible."

And then I had it.

I really did.

I smiled. "I love this," I said.

He smiled back at me. "You're good, Izzy."

I couldn't help it. I burst out: "Sure. You were going to take your kayak and leave me."

He shook his head. "I wanted to feel the water, to see what it was like. I knew there wasn't room for both of us, and I was trying to think of what to do."

I thought about it. "All right." And then we smiled again.

It was dawn as we tied up the kayak. "All right," he said.

"All right," I echoed.

I glanced up at the sky. It was dark with birds coming toward the island. Coming back to nest? Was it spring?

Please let it be spring.

FORTY-FIVE

MATT

IZZY sat across from me, in the teacher's house, her hair in knots. Too bad she didn't have a comb. But then, neither did I. Her hands rested on Willie's broad head.

Izzy, that mosquito, paddled really well. Could we make the trip together?

I must have said it aloud.

"We have to try," she said. "You can do it, Matt. I'm not worried about that. And I can do it too."

I almost laughed. Izzy had no idea of what it would be like: storms brewing, flipping over.

She had no idea of how we would right ourselves.

I looked down at her dog. Willie's eyes were shut. He was stretched out, comfortable, not realizing what danger we were in.

"What can we do about the dog?" I asked her.

Izzy pushed at her glasses. I noticed a small part of a lens had fallen out. She looked even stranger than usual.

Her hand was raised over the dog's back now. "What are you talking about?"

"I hate to leave him."

"Of course I won't leave him. He'd starve without me." She stopped. "We belong together. In all this time..." She didn't finish.

"There's no room."

"Certainly there's room. We'll squish together. Willie and me. That's the way it has to be."

"Stop tapping your foot for once," I said, shaking my head. What difference did it make if we took the kayak out and headed away? It might never work anyway. We might be back here in hours.

And then what?

"All right," I said, knowing I could never have left my own dog to starve. I could never leave any dog to starve!

As soon as we had a clear day, we went to the cove. I carried the bits and pieces of food we had left. I wedged them under my seat in the kayak, saying, "You get in first. Sit down and I'll hand Willie to you."

She looked worried. "He's pretty heavy."

I didn't answer. What was the use? I hauled the dog up, his legs scrambling against my chest, and managed to drop him into the kayak on Izzy's lap.

"Nothing to it," she said.

But the dog looked terrified as the boat rocked in the water.

I gave Izzy a paddle and slid into the kayak.

It was a perfect day, and we could see that the island was smudged with green. It really was spring. But the water was rougher than usual, the waves high.

Izzy dipped her paddle in too gently; she just wasn't strong enough for this, even though she was trying hard. She'd be better off rowing on the Sound. As if that would ever happen.

She stopped paddling and looked at a gull.

It swooped down over the water and came up with a small fish in its mouth.

"Bonaparte's gull," she said with satisfaction.

She'd been looking through her mom's bird book most of the time we were stuck in the cave. I'd watched her moving her lips, repeating birds' names. That, or lips still moving, reading *The Call of the Wild,* a book I'd read about four times. Sometimes, her head bent, she'd write.

Pay attention, I told myself fiercely as the kayak turned on its own. "Hey, Izzy," I added. "Paddle!"

"Sorry," she said.

We didn't talk then; keeping the boat facing the waves took up all our energy. And for Izzy, there was the added weight of Willie, who was panting, trembling.

We heard the thunder of the plane before we saw it. It flew low over us, and even lower over the island.

We looked up, shading our eyes. Still, we couldn't see. I thought I saw the round red circle of the enemy.

It was a good thing we were only a dot in the water, with waves spilling over the sides of the kayak, soaking us.

"Paddle faster," I told Izzy, even though I knew she was doing the best she could. Then, "Sorry."

I thought of Pop, his blue eyes, the beard he'd grown when we first got here. If I ever saw him again, I'd tell him . . . tell him how much like him I was.

If only he were here, my grouchy, grumpy father.

How different it all would have been.

FORTY-SIX

Izzy

THE sound of the plane must have frightened Willie. He struggled in my arms; his claws dug into the side of the kayak.

I tried to hold him, but he dove over the edge and was in the water. He paddled away from me, waves hitting his head, waves that would be too much for him.

I looked back at Matt, terrified. "We have to go after him!" I yelled. "We have to go back. Please..."

I didn't see him nod; I didn't hear him say anything, but he pulled hard on the paddle, turning us, and I dug hard at my own paddle until we were next to the dog, close to the island, the boom of the surf in our ears.

Willie's paws looked so large on land, but in the water he was almost defenseless, trying to fight the current...

Until a wave pushed him along, up and up, tossing him onto the sandy shore, and our kayak scraped bottom moments later.

Out of breath, I climbed out of the boat, smashing onto the sand, drenched and scraped. I reached out to the dog, who lay next to me, panting.

I took a quick glance around to see what Matt was doing. He was pulling the kayak up along the sand, close to us. "We're not going to let this one get away," he said.

I coughed and managed to nod against a pale sun in my eyes.

Matt stood over me. "Are you all right?" His gloves were soaked. He shook his hands to get them off. And I did the same thing.

Willie was up now, shaking himself. Icy droplets flew across the sand.

"Oh, Willie," I said, and then, "Oh, Matt."

What would we do now? We could never have tried it again with the dog in the boat, and even though we'd been out less than an hour, I realized I couldn't try it again myself.

FORTY-SEVEN

MATT

OVERHEAD, I heard the thunder of planes. I looked up. Americans, at last.

We were safe, but only for the moment. We had to get away from the village. And we had to go by tomorrow.

We hadn't seen the four soldiers, but they might be here somewhere.

I had to think. How to move, how to leave.

Even for spring, it was cold. We needed coats, gloves, blankets.

What about food? Was there enough still in the kayak to get us through? I had to gather mussels from the pier pilings before we left. And maybe crabs scuttling along the sand. So we had to stay near the water, but still be able to gather eggs from the gulls' nests.

But the hardest thing was shelter!

How could we survive outside?

Izzy was watching me. "Towels first." Her lips were blue with cold, and she was shivering.

We went back to the village, the dog still shaking off water, and went up the steps to my house, quietly, watching.

I pulled dirty towels off the hooks in the bathroom and we wrapped ourselves in them. Izzy knelt on the floor, rubbing the dog down until his fur was dry and gleaming. "We'll be all right," she said. But I heard the fear in her voice.

I couldn't waste time worrying. *Food,* I told myself again as I listened uneasily to the sound of planes overhead.

I zipped up my jacket, still damp. My stomach was turning over with hunger. It was getting late, and we had to have something to eat tonight. "I'll be back," I said. "I want to check the pier pilings for mussels."

Willie's ribs were showing, curved under the fur. I had to find something for him too.

And we had to leave.

It was our only hope.

FORTY-EIGHT

Izzy

I stopped shivering at last, and Matt was back with mussels. Then something tugged at my mind. Something about Maria.

Poor Maria, so far away. Would I ever see her again?

But what was it? Then I remembered. That day on Thor Hill. What had she said? *Just an overhang under the rocks, but cozy.* She'd waved her hand. *The other side of Thor Hill.*

At least, something like that.

I grabbed Matt's arm. "I know where we can go. It's not far, but I think it may be safe. And we might be able to find it."

He looked up, really listening. "Are you sure?"

"Sure!" A mussel slid down my throat. "We have to gather everything together and go!"

FORTY-NINE

MATT

I hardly listened to the rest of what she was saying. I was thinking ahead. She could walk with Willie; I could take the kayak, the front cockpit filled with everything warm we had.

I kept nodding at her, at that mess of a girl, who might be saving our lives.

"Yes," I said. "Oh, yes," because I realized it must be on the side of the cove I had found first.

Not too far. At home, I would have thought it was impossibly far. But we could do this.

I was glad we had a plan, something that was possible. At least something to try.

Again, we went from house to house. A large red scarf under someone's bed. A quilt rolled up behind someone's couch. A warm glove, just one, under someone's table.

And that was it.

Before dawn, I shoved everything warm we had into the kayak. With the food, it was piled high. If the kayak turned over...

I couldn't think of that.

In the early morning, before light, we were ready to go.

FIFTY

Izzy

WE left when it was still dark. I waved at Matt as he headed toward the harbor.

"Come on, Willie," I said. "It's time to go."

The dog looked up at me, considering, but I patted his head, and he decided he'd come with me.

We stayed away from the path and walked along the edge of the field. Even though it was still cold, green covered the earth, and there was the constant sound of birds.

Ahead of me, Thor Hill rose up against the sky, Gulls circled in the wisps of mist, and I thought again about that day with Maria, long ago.

Planes went overhead steadily and once, I heard the explosion of what must have been a bomb. The sound was faint, so not the village. Not yet.

Willie and I circled the hill and reached the other

side while it was still light. I had to find that overhang. So many rocks. So many places to search.

But a miracle. Matt was there ahead of me, yelling something above the surf, pointing.

And there it was, just under the shadow of the hill, protected. Almost a cave, but not quite. An overhang, exactly. We could anchor blankets on the sides to keep out the wind. And there would be just enough room for the three of us, covered with scarves and blankets, Matt and me wearing our coats.

We could do it.

But Matt was looking at the sky. It was almost dark with planes now. So many of them.

"American," I breathed. "At last, ours."

He looked at me irritably. "American bombs could kill us just as well."

He was miserable.

I turned away from him and began to cover the sides with blankets, weighing everything down with rocks.

FIFTY-ONE

MATT

I should have said I was sorry. I opened my mouth a few times, but she paid no attention. "Good job with the sides," I said, and helped her wedge the last rocks against the blankets.

She didn't answer. And after the sides were secure, she crawled underneath and curled up with Willie almost on top of her.

I sat outside, listening to the blankets flap. The white one blended in, but the blue one really would have stood out, if it hadn't been covered by rocks. I hoped it might not be seen from the sky.

I thought about today. I'd been lucky, first because the waves were gentle, the trip was easy, except...

"Except what?" Izzy's voice was muffled; she was still turned away from me.

"I was talking aloud?"

"I don't read minds, after all," she said.

"I was thinking about the planes overhead, going south. It could be the battle the Japanese soldier talked about," I said slowly.

She was sitting up now, facing me. Was she crying?

"Are you afraid?" I asked.

"Sure," she said.

But it wasn't that, we were afraid all the time. I knew it was because of me.

I didn't stop to think. I crawled underneath the overhang and sat there with Willie between us. And now I did say it. "I'm sorry, Izzy."

She didn't stop crying. She cried even more. "Izzy the Mosquito," I said. "You're my best friend."

And that was true.

She laughed through her tears. "I'm your only friend."

I didn't laugh, though. I thought of all she had done these long months. How could I have made it without her?

I reached across Willie and took her hand.

"On the ship," she said. "I'm clumsy. I never meant..."

"I know you didn't do it on purpose. I should have

known it all along. And someday," I said, "we'll be home. We'll go out on the Sound together."

"Home!" She squeezed my hand. "Willie too. And the Sound!"

I felt tears in my throat. I couldn't let her see that. Instead, I just nodded.

FIFTY-TWO

Izzy

WE finally saw the ships on the horizon one day. And it wasn't long before bombs rained down and shots were fired.

The noise vibrated in my ears and chest. Willie hated it as much as I did, whining, then howling.

It was all coming closer. But still, we had to have food.

"We have to climb the hill and look for nests," I told Matt, covering my ears against the boom of the battle.

He looked doubtful, but shrugged. "No worse up there, maybe."

We climbed, heads down, looking for nests in the rocks, but we couldn't find any. "Maybe it's too soon," I said, not sure if he could hear me.

Below, there was a tremendous boom.

"We have to do something," Matt said when we

reached the overhang again and climbed in for what little bit of warmth it gave us.

"They'll think the enemy might be here," I said, knowing what he meant and feeling my heart pound.

I remembered a movie I'd seen with Gram. Something about a man marooned on an island, dragging rocks on the sand that spelled out SOS. *Save Our Souls.*

But how would American fliers know we were on their side? Suppose we were the enemy?

I thought I knew a better way.

I leaned close to Matt's ear. "Listen. If we take the blankets, the blue one, the white one..." I broke off, trying to think. "The large red scarf." Yes "Can you hear me?"

"Yes. Then what?"

"We'll anchor them down with rocks on top of the hill. Red, white, and blue. The Americans will know friends are here."

He shook his head. I knew he was thinking that without the blankets we'd be freezing.

A huge explosion that raised smoke in the air convinced him.

We went back to the top of the hill, carrying the

blankets and the scarf, and spread everything out in order. Red, white, and blue, a huge flag, all weighed down so it would stay in place.

Fliers would see it; maybe they wouldn't bomb. They might even wonder who was here and come to get us.

In the meantime, we'd manage to huddle together, me, Matt, and Willie.

Later, from the overhang, I saw a bird with a yellow back and a soft buff color below. Its legs were long and yellow too.

I thought of the picture Dad had drawn long ago: the yellow bittern. It was the one I'd seen a couple of times, a rare bird that must have flown all the way from Indonesia.

The bird turned and stared at me. He dipped his head, then spread his wings slowly and flew. I watched until he was only a dot in the sky and then disappeared.

If only Mom were here.

If only she could see. A yellow bittern!

I'd write about that bird, though, and tell her someday.

FIFTY-THREE

MATT

SOMETIMES planes flew over, loud and vibrating, but we were never bombed. Izzy said it was because of her flag.

It was a great flag, so I never mentioned that most of the time it was hidden in the fog.

Would the war ever end? Would Pop and Izzy's mom come back?

Would we ever go home?

One morning, there were no bombs, only the *rat-tat-tat* of the guns went on. Izzy pointed to a flock of birds flying in from the sea and crawled out to see them.

I watched her running along after them, head up, stumbling on the sand with Willie; then they disappeared behind the rocks.

She was gone a long time, too long. I'd have to go after her and make sure she was all right.

I went along the sand, back around the hill, and she was there, arms out, crying. "Oh, Matt!" she called.

And I noticed that the sound of the firing had stopped.

FIFTY-FOUR

Izzy

I fell, pushed myself up, and went on. I was crying, sobbing, yelling Matt's name. Willie ran with me. Did he know? Did he have any idea?

The voice behind me kept calling, "Wait! Stop!"

I couldn't wait; I couldn't stop.

Matt came toward me. "What is it, Izzy? What's the matter?"

I ran straight into his arms, crying hard, but still managing to say, "Look, dear Matt. Look."

Willie tore around us, barking; he knew something had happened. Of course he did.

Matt kept looking down at me. "Are you all right?"

I couldn't say anything more. I raised my hand and pointed over my shoulder.

And then he saw: the blue uniform, the smiling face of the man behind me. A sailor from an American ship.

"I've come to take you home," he said, and his arms were out too.

FIFTY-FIVE

MATT

I couldn't cry, not with that sailor smiling, nodding at us.

But when he said, "We saw the flag, and now we've won the battle..." I really did cry: Izzy and I hugging each other.

I was going home to Connecticut, to Mom, to rowing on the Sound.

And Izzy?

I was used to the way she looked, the way she tapped her feet. She'd roll her eyes when I was grumpy, and sometimes she made me laugh.

I really would take her out on the Sound. I knew she'd love it. And we'd wait together for Pop and her mom to come home.

"What about the dog?" the sailor asked.

We looked at each other, then looked at him. "We don't leave without the dog," I said.

FIFTY-SIX

Izzy

IT was warm, the backyard filled with color, the hall clock chiming, a half-eaten chocolate cake on the counter.

I was home at last!

I held hands with Gram across the kitchen table. Her hair was gray now, and her face lined, but I thought she was beautiful.

And Willie? Underneath on my feet, chewing on a huge bone. Willie thought he was in heaven.

I thought so too.

For a moment, Gram and I were quiet, thinking about Mom, Matt's father, Maria, Mrs. Weio, and the others who had been taken from the island. I ran my hand over the bracelet still on my wrist.

"We have to believe they'll come home too," Gram said.

I did believe it. Someday, Mom would sit here just the way I was sitting.

"I'm so glad to be here," I said, feeling sorry. "Dad thought I'd love the island best, but..."

She patted my hand. "Wait, Izzy."

She went into Dad's old office and came back with photos. One showed the front of our house, another our kitchen table with a roast turkey in the center, and still a third, me sitting on a swing out back. "He was so glad to be home, Izzy."

She pushed a book across the table. *Coming Home,* the title read.

I could read it, read all of his books now. A little slowly maybe, carefully. But yes, what would I have done without Maria's books?

Then I remembered something. I patted Gram's hand, slid my feet from under Willie, and went into my bedroom.

Mom's water-stained notebook was still in my suitcase. I ran my hand over it. It had been with Matt and me the whole time.

I brought it back to Gram and we sat paging through it together. The last half was in my writing: wild and loopy, even though I'd thought it was my best. I'd written about the yellow bittern staring at me with round dark eyes, rain spattering across the rocks, the kayak, and...

I stopped. The island was so clear, the wind bending us sideways, the snow slanting, an irritable boy who'd become my best friend.

Gram looked at me, smiling. "You see it."

I could hardly breathe. I did see it. I had captured the island, page after page: that wild, windswept, desolate place.

I was a writer.

How had that happened?

You could do anything if only you'd set your mind to it.

Oh, Mrs. Dane. I'd tell her about it. No, I'd write it for her. And rowing on the Sound someday with Matt. Willie's new life. And mine.

I'd write it all.

I couldn't wait to begin.

A NOTE:

This is a work of fiction, but always there's a kernel of truth in the writing. And so it is with *Island War*.

The story is loosely based on the island of Attu, the farthest west in the chain of the Aleutian Islands, eleven hundred miles from the mainland part of Alaska. It is windswept, with only eight to ten clear days a year free from rain, snow, and fog.

The small island was inhabited by the Aleuts, who hunted and fished for a living. Birds fly there in remarkable numbers, many not seen anywhere else on this continent.

During the Second World War, Attu and Kiska were the only territories of the United States invaded by the Japanese army. On Attu, everyone from the small village was taken off the island, and sent to Japan. At the end of the war, only half were alive, but they were never permitted to return to their homes. They were forced to settle elsewhere in Alaska.

For many years, birders came to the island, which had been taken over by the government. The battlefield became a national landmark.

But suppose, I thought, as I began to write this book, a boy and a girl remained on the island to survive on their own?

ACKNOWLEDGMENTS

I owe much to my editor, Mary Cash, for her belief in me, for her thoughtful editing, and wonderful suggestions. I'm grateful too, for my long association and friendship with Terry Borzumato, and for Barbara Perris's careful copyediting.

As always, Joan Jansen was more than willing to help with research and added to my thoughts about the book.

My daughter, Alice, and my son, Bill, are always there for me, both tremendous sources of encouragement and love. Laurie Giff, my daughter-in-law, and I have been through much together, and urge each other on.

My seven wonderful grandchildren, Jimmy, Chrissy, Bill, Cait, Conor, Patti, and Jilli, as well as Cathie Giff, Bill's wife, and Jim O'Meara, Alice's husband, have added so much to our family, and are willing to read my books!

I'm especially indebted to E. Andrew Duda for his enormous support and advice over the years.

I particularly want to mention my sister-in-law, Mary Giff, who is so dear to me. Our weekly talks, our memories of family, and her knowledge of my books make me want to keep writing and writing.